Kattie
II may the Road
Rise up to meet you
K

Code Name Sonny:
Book One of the Code Name Series

K.E. Pottie

BookLocker
Saint Petersburg, Florida

Print ISBN: 978-1-64719-304-1
Epub ISBN: 978-1-64719-305-8
Mobi ISBN: 978-1-64719-306-5

Published by BookLocker.com, Inc., St. Petersburg, Florida.

The characters and events in this book are fictitious. Any similarity to real persons, living or dead, is coincidental and not intended by the author.

Printed on acid-free paper.

Booklocker.com, Inc.
2021

First Edition

Library of Congress Cataloguing in Publication Data
Pottie, K.E.
Code Name Sonny: Book One of the Code Name Series by K.E. Pottie
Library of Congress Control Number: 2021900155

Dedication

This book is dedicated to Laren "Sonny" Pottie
July 2nd, 1927 – November 2nd, 2012
RIP Dad, we love you.

Contents

Introduction

Appeal by General de Gaulle to the French
18 June 1940[1]
The leaders, who, for many years past, have been at the head of the French armed forces, have set up a government.

Alleging the defeat of our armies, this government has entered into negotiations with the enemy with a view to bringing about a cessation of hostilities. It is quite true that we were, and still are, overwhelmed by enemy mechanized forces, both on the ground and in the air. It was the tanks, the planes, and the tactics of the Germans, far more than the fact that we were outnumbered, that forced our armies to retreat. It was the German tanks, planes, and tactics that provided the element of surprise, which brought our leaders to their present plight.

But has the last word been said? Must we abandon all hope? Is our defeat final and irremediable? To these questions I answer—No!

Speaking in full knowledge of the facts, I ask you to believe me when I say that the cause of France is not lost. The very factors that brought about our defeat may one day lead us to victory.

For, remember this, France does not stand-alone. She is not isolated. Behind her are a vast Empire and she can make common cause with the British Empire, which commands the seas and is continuing the struggle. Like England, she can draw unreservedly on the immense industrial resources of the United States.

This war is not limited to our unfortunate country. The outcome of the struggle has not been decided by the Battle of

---

1 *The War Memoirs of Charles De Gaulle: Volume One: The Call to Honor*, 1940-1942, by Charles de Gaulle, translated by Jonathan Griffin.

France. This is a world war. Mistakes have been made, there have been delays and untold suffering, but the fact remains that there still exists in the world everything we need to crush our enemies someday. Today we are crushed by the sheer weight of mechanized force hurled against us, but we can still look to a future in which even greater mechanized force will bring us victory. The destiny of the world is at stake.

I, General de Gaulle, now in London, call on all French officers and men who are at present on British soil, or may be in the future, with or without their arms; I call on all engineers and skilled workmen from the armaments factories who are at present on British soil, or may be in the future, to get in touch with me.

Whatever happens, the flame of French resistance must not and shall not die.

Spy!

It was a spring day in 1944 when Joe and Raymond raced each other through the school's front gate moments after the closing school bell rang. The sun felt warm on their skin, but as they made their way downtown, chilly gusts reminded them that shards of winter were still in the air. It was still not warm enough to go outdoors without their winter coats; that time of year when you need to carry one, just in case.

Weather wasn't top of mind for the two friends today. They were on a special mission that afternoon: They wanted to be the first to discover what was causing the biggest buzz of excitement they could recall in their quiet town.

The FBI had arrested the owner of the French River Inn, Mr. Leopold von Sliedricht, a suspected Nazi spy. Sliedricht was a White Russian who hired Jewish workers at his establishment, so no one in town ever suspected a traitor in their midst.

The FBI had been tracking von Sliedricht's activities and correspondence for months. They worked on a series of tips they had received from von Sliedricht's disgruntled wife.

The boys turned on to Lincoln Street, coats open to the wind, hair flying, heaving breath casting frosty explosions as they dodged cars and leaped over potholes, too excited even to speak.

They glanced at each other in silent disbelief that World War II had encroached on their sleepy New England town.

Joe and Raymond skidded to a halt at a makeshift roadblock that kept cars and pedestrians from the scene. Town police stood at guard behind wooden barriers that they had erected there from the townsfolk's workshops and barns.

Behind the police line, eleven men in dark suits and hats carrying Tommy guns were directing army personnel with mine detectors, poking at the bushes around the establishment, and raising cellar doors at the back of the tavern. Meanwhile, a steady stream of State Guardsmen moved in and out of the inn's front entrance, carrying crates to two waiting army trucks, where they stacked them row upon row. Six army soldiers with rifles kept a watchful eye over the loading operation.

The news of the FBI arrest was traveling fast, and the boys grinned with delight at their front row seats, watching in silence as an FBI agent shoved Mr. von Sliedricht headfirst into a black Packard sedan, his hands in cuffs behind his back.

"Get a look at that! They've got him in handcuffs! Guess he must be dangerous," Raymond whispered to Joe.

"Like you could tell," Joe retorted with a snort, only to receive the evil eye from Raymond for drawing attention.

Two FBI agents, wearing big badges and fedoras, turned to stare at the boys. The agents spoke with each other for a few moments before one strode over to the barrier.

He beckoned Joe and Raymond to come forward.

"You boys familiar with Mr. von Sliedricht?" he asked.

"Yes." Both boys mumbled, awed by their first sight at a G-Man.

"Have you seen anyone not from around here come to visit him?" the agent asked.

Raymond shook his head no. But Joe hesitated.

"Spit it out boy! What did you see?" the FBI agent ordered.

"A few times I spotted this doozy of a car, a maroon Nash Ambassador with a New York license plate, parked in the lot next to the French River Inn.

"Do you get a good look at the driver or passenger?" the agent asked.

"The driver was a tall older man with eyeglasses, dressed in a tweed gray jacket and wool trousers," Joe said. "Mr. von Sliedricht came out of the inn to greet them."

"What did the passenger look like?" the agent asked.

She was a young blond woman dressed like a movie star," Joe said. "She was a babe."

His face turned red.

"Fascinating," said the agent, as he pulled out his pen and a yellow pad and began writing notes on the pad.

The FBI agent rattled off more questions to Joe.

"Can you recall any specific dates when they were here?"

"How often were they in town?"

"How long did they stay?"

Joe felt his hands and forehead perspire. The questions terrified him. His stomach was churning, brain spinning, heart pounding. He felt like he couldn't breathe.

I'm in big trouble with Mom over this, for sure, he thought. *But I might be in bigger trouble with this FBI agent if I don't tell him everything I learned.*

Joe told the FBI agent everything he could remember; his confession delivered in a rush.

"I saw them maybe about eight or nine times this year in February, March, and three times around Easter. The first time was early February. I was walking to Woolworths and had never seen a car like that before. The other times, I was on my bike running an errand for my Mom and I remember thinking: there's that chrome beauty with the New York license plate back at the French River Inn," Joe said.

"That's quite a memory you have, kid," the agent said.

"I am told I have a photographic memory," Joe said.

"It serves you well," the agent said. "How long did they stay?"

"I figured it was relatives or some friends of theirs, because they stayed a few days each time," Joe said.

"Did you see anyone else with the couple besides Mr. Sliedricht?" the FBI agent asked.

"Just Mr. von Slie…" Joe started to say but changed his mind.

"Are you sure?" the agent said, noting his hesitation.

"Now that you mention it, the property caretakers seemed to be around them too," Joe replied.

"Do you think the man and woman from New York are spies too?" Raymond chirped in.

"You never know, young man, you never know," the FBI agent said, patting the boys on their heads as thanks. He turned on his heels and strode back into the inn.

Three FBI agents emerged through the tavern's cellar door, each carrying four MP 40 German submachine guns. The FBI formed a protective barrier around the incriminating evidence.

The FBI agent who interrogated the boys turned to James Kenney, one of the local police officers, and ordered him to secure the area.

Scanning the scene, Officer Kenney yelled to the boys, "You kids get outta here. This area is under official FBI quarantine—now go home!"

The boys kicked at broken pavement as they walked away, disappointed at being ejected just when things were getting ripe with excitement.

"I guess that guy who was questioning us is the honcho of this operation," Joe said, grinning at the honor of making his acquaintance.

"Like Officer Kenney would know how to be an FBI agent!" Raymond complained under his breath. The boys giggled at Raymond's jibe at Officer Kenney as they walked home. While chagrined they couldn't stay, they were still proud to have had a front row view of the only historical event they could recall happening in their Podunk village.

Joe and Raymond talked nonstop as they headed home along Route 27, stopping to argue about whether Mr. von

Sliedricht was a spy, or just being picked on because he was White Russian, because everyone knew White Russians are sympathetic to the Nazi cause. Their serious conversation gave way to talk about that night's radio shows, followed by griping that two girls at school, Cynthia and Lois, still wouldn't give them the time of day. The conversation led to what homework they had to finish.

"I'm famished," Joe announced, walking faster. "I wonder what Mom's made for dinner. Dinner! Yikes! They were late for dinner.

The friends looked at each other. There would be hell to pay! They ran as fast as they could, but they arrived at their separate homes more than an hour past their suppertime.

"Where have you been, Sonny?" his mother asked Joe, using her nickname for him since his birth. "Supper's cold and you've kept your brothers and sister waiting," she greeted him as he closed the front door behind him.

"Sorry, Mom; we ran downtown to see what was going on with Mr. von Sliedricht. Did you hear the FBI arrested him?" Joe replied. He lowered his book strap to the floor, removed his coat, and hung it up on the wall in the foyer.

"Yes, I heard," she said, sighing, and walked back to the kitchen with Joe following behind her. "I think it's awful they are on a spy hunt. I don't suppose that nice man would do anything to hurt our little town or our country," she replied.

"Mom, Nazi spies don't all run around wearing black uniforms and swastikas. We saw with our own eyes what happened today at the French River Inn. They found a huge stash of German machine guns and all kinds of weapons at Mr. von Sliedricht's place. They hauled off crates and crates of ammo in two army trucks!" Joe blurted with excitement.

"I want you to stay away from there, Sonny! Promise me you won't go snooping around that inn while the FBI is in town."

"But..."

"No buts—promise me Sonny!"

"Ok, I will."

With a shrug, Joe continued into the dining room to take his seat at the table. His two older brothers, Armand and Clarence, gave him dirty looks for keeping them waiting. His sister Louise kicked him under the table as payback for her sharp hunger pangs.

After dinner that night, Raymond and Joe went to their favorite fishing hole, which was on von Sliedricht's property. The boys saw no harm in such an adventure. They were no threat to von Sliedricht, and it was in a far corner of his property. They sat down on a log by the water's edge, preparing their fishing poles.

"Think the fish are biting tonight?" Raymond said.

"I hope so," Sonny replied. "I brought our secret bait with me tonight."

"What secret bait?" Raymond asked.

"Corn."

"Corn?" Raymond asked. "You think that will work?"

"Clarence says so," Joe said.

"Your brother thinks he knows everything," Raymond said. "I betcha it doesn't work!"

"You're on," Joe said. "Whoever catches a fish first, the other guy has to carry his books to school for a week."

"It's a wager then," Raymond said.

Joe attached some corn to the hook, while Raymond used a night crawler. After a few minutes, Joe had a nice sized fish on his hook. He dangled it in front of Raymond.

"Pure luck, Joe" Raymond said. "I'd bet you can't do that twice."

Joe didn't reveal he had come here after school, feeding the fish corn for the past few weeks. He would enjoy watching Raymond carry his books for him!

Just as Joe was about to toss his corn-laden line into the water, they heard a voice come from the woods behind them.

"How's the fishing, boys?" a man said in a deep tone.

They looked around, terrified, when a man as dark as the evening stepped out from the tree line. Joe and Raymond couldn't decide is they wanted to jump into the lake or run like hell. They ran like hell. Leaving their fishing poles behind, they bolted into the forest, to the laughter of the dark man.

"Who was that?" Joe said as they ran through branches and brambles without regard.

"I don't know, but I never saw him before!" Raymond said. "Just keep moving, or he'll catch us."

They emerged onto the main road leading to home. Looking behind them, and not seeing the dark man follow, they stopped running.

Joe halted, "Our poles are back there. Should we go back and get them?"

"No way am I going back there," Raymond said. "That guy will kill us!"

"That was Clarence's fishing pole," Joe said. "If I lose that he will kill me!"

"We can go back tomorrow after school," Raymond said. "Our stuff should still be there."

"Okay, but cover me if Clarence asks," Joe said.

"What do you want me to say?" Raymond asked.

"I don't know, just make something up!" Joe said.

"Sure thing buddy," Raymond said. "I'll just tell him some Nazi spies chased us through the woods."

"It does sound crazy," Joe said. "I just hope he's not home."

When they arrived back at the house, it relieved Joe to see that Clarence wasn't home yet.

"Sonny, what happened to you? You're a mess!" his mom said.

"We were out fishing tonight mom," Joe said. "Is Clarence home yet?"

"No, he is out running an errand for me," Emma said. "If you went fishing, where is your fishing pole?"

"We forgot it at the pond," Joe lied. "Can I go lay down? I am not feeling so good, Mom."

Emma did not press him to explain why he would leave his fishing pole at the pond. Then she saw his in the corner in the foyer.

"If your brother finds out you lost his fishing pole, he'll be furious at you," Emma said.

"I know, Mom," Joe said. "Can you please cover for me? I promise I'll get it back tomorrow. Clarence won't know it was ever missing."

"Okay, Sonny," Emma said. "But next time keep your head on your shoulders and think!"

"Sure, Mom," Joe said, giving her a kiss on the cheek. He went in his bedroom and hid under his covers.

Later that night Emma brought her Sonny-Boy a glass of warm milk.

***

Early the next morning Joe awoke to the smell of bacon and coffee wafting up from the kitchen. He rolled out of bed, noticing that the old hand-me-down mattress had caved in the middle. He bounded down the stairs in his pajamas and threw himself onto a chair at the table.

"Morning, Sonny. Hungry?" his Mom grinned.

"Ravenous!" Joe said as he smiled back.

"There's coffee on the table. Careful; it's steaming, and the bacon will be ready by and by. Help yourself to the toast."

Joe wolfed down his breakfast in a matter of minutes, sparking remarks from his mother about "watching his table manners" and "where did you learn to eat like that?"

"I'm in a hurry, Mom. We have a science lab this morning and I want to get in a little early to set up."

"I'm glad you're so dedicated to your schoolwork, Sonny. We are all very proud you're graduating at seventeen!" his mother remarked.

"Did I get any letters from the universities yet?" Sonny asked.

"No dear, nothing yet."

"Think I can get into an Ivy League college?"

"You can do anything you set your heart on, Sonny-boy," she said.

Joe blew an appreciative kiss, threw his coat over his arm, grabbed his book strap, and started out the door.

"Oh, and Sonny, please pick up your radio parts in the living room when you get home, you've made such a mess on the coffee table and all over the floor. One of your brothers or your sister is likely to trip on them."

"Okay, Mom, I will," was Joe's quick reply as he shut the door, ran down the steps of his duplex, and bounded up the steps of the duplex next door. Joe and Raymond's moms worked at the cloth factory in town, and like most factory workers, they lived in duplexes within walking distance of the factory.

Joe knocked on Raymond's door and he appeared, wearing his heavy winter coat.

"Why are you wearing that coat?" Joe asked, "It's not that cold out."

"Because of this," Raymond said grinning, opening his coat to display a vial.

"What is that?" Joe asked.

"It's a stink bomb," Raymond replied.

"I will not pull this prank with you," Joe said. "School is almost out, and it's our final lab test. I'm trying to get into an Ivy League college, not get expelled from high school."

"C'mon, you're no fun, Joe, it's a senior tradition. Besides, you're Mrs. Hamilton's pet. Our science teacher would never suspect you," laughed Raymond.

"Just keep me out of this," grimaced Joe.

"Okay buddy, when I'm *in like Flynn* with Cynthia and Lois, remember I offered you the chance."

"Let's go, Raymond," Joe said. "I don't want to be late."

The friends began their two-mile walk to school, passing the time with banter and teasing.

When the boys entered the science lab, Raymond moved over to one of the floor vents and removed the screws with a pocketknife. He lifted off the vent cover and peered inside, clearing out the cobwebs and dust. He set the cover on Mrs. Hamilton's desk and moved to their lab bench.

Raymond removed a vial of chemicals from the cabinet. He uncorked it and poured it into his vial, covering the latter with a small, thin piece of paper. He placed his vial on a ledge in the vent, replacing the vent cover and tightening the screws. He squinted into the vent and smiled when he recognized the vial was still in place.

"This is pure genius," Raymond declared.

"The school maintenance man doesn't turn on the boiler until everybody is here and he'll shut it off the minute frugal Principal Lewis says so. When the furnace kicks on during class, the vial will fall into the ventilation system, stinking up the whole building, and we'll get out of school. Thank me in advance for a day off, Joe."

Joe walked to the door and peered down the corridor to make sure Raymond's antics hadn't attracted attention.

"I still don't condone the idea, but a day off would be nice," Joe mused. "Betcha the trout are biting."

"About time you came around," admonished Raymond.

"Are you sure they can't pin this on us?" Joe asked, still worried.

"If G-men are still hanging around," Raymond proclaimed. "They'd be the only ones smart enough to figure it out."

Less than an hour later, Mrs. Hamilton led the class out onto the school grounds, her scarf wadded in a ball covering her mouth and nose.

A cold breeze blew across the group of students and teachers.

"It smells as if the sewers in town backed up," she cried, a strange look of disgust coupled with a perplexed frown on her face.

Raymond and Joe giggled as they exited the building, coughing and gagging, too.

Later that day, the school's science lab stars stood in the Principal's office denying responsibility for the prank.

During the four years that Joe and Raymond had lived next door to each other, they had adopted a routine of sneaking out of their bedroom windows to the side rooftop overhang at night.

They sat for hours quizzing each other with their knowledge of constellations, moon cycles, automobiles, radios, baseball, and girls. They dreamed what they'd do when they both became rich and famous; Joe as a doctor and Raymond pitching in Major League baseball, playing with the likes of Joe DiMaggio, Ted Williams, Stan Musial, and Bobby Doerr.

Raymond arranged their rooftop rendezvous by tapping Morse code on the wall separating the duplexes. Over time, the wall plaster fell on his bed from the constant rapping. His mother was mystified at the curious case of deteriorating plaster, until they caught Raymond tapping on the wall one night. That incident broke their Morse code routine. Still, their nightly rendezvous continued.

As the boys walked home from school, they prearranged a time to meet on the roof after dinner.

Joe and Raymond enjoyed their impromptu day off from school with six hours of trout fishing. That cool fall evening, when they convened for their nightly conversation on the rooftop, they were too tired to do much more than laugh at the looks of horror on the faces of Mrs. Hamilton, Principal Lewis, and Cynthia and Lois, the stuck-up girls in high school. They retired to their beds, pleased as punch to have carried out the school's annual prank unscathed.

Raymond instigated most of the pranks at school, with Joe as his faithful accomplice. But Joe's prank achieved the most notoriety, because it remained unsolved during his entire life: He built a homemade radio that blocked out the local radio station.

The odd incident of the eleven hours of radio silence was the matter of conversations in taverns, shops and at dinner tables for months afterward.

Joe's mom and sister had suspected his involvement because the radio blackout happened just two days after Joe removed his radio parts from the end table and floor in the den and took them up to his bedroom.

The Revelation

It was 9 p.m. when Jack and Emily drove up in their Toyota Highlander to pick up Jack's parents for a New Year's Eve dance at the local Elks Club. They celebrated New Year's Eve with four couples their own age, but Jack's dad had again offered that he had two "extra" tickets to the Elks Club festivities.

This year, Emily said, "What the heck, it might be fun to do something different."

Truth was, in prior years, Jack's parents always had spare tickets, but by the time they asked, Jack and Emily had already committed to celebrating with their friends. But this was the eve of a new millennium— December 31, 1999—and everyone agreed it would fit to ring it in by celebrating the milestone as a family.

"Happy New Year," Joe greeted them in the hallway. "Your mother has appetizers ready for us before we leave to the club for the dance."

The aroma of baked Brie and smoked sausage directed them to the den.

"Smells delicious, Mom," Emily complimented as she walked ahead to greet Claire, her mother-in-law. They hugged each other, pirouetted to show off their party dresses, and were talking when Joe and Jack joined them.

My son and I got lucky, Joe thought. *These two charming ladies proposed to us!*

"Highball?" he asked Jack.

"No, but I'll take a beer," Jack replied.

"Sure, grab one from the fridge," Joe said as he leaned over to pick at the Brie, but Claire slapped his hand away. "Get plates, dear," she said as she opened a drawer and set out small forks and knives. Jack laughed at his parents' familiar playful nature as he popped the top from his beer bottle and took a healthy swig.

The mood was festive as they joked, stuffing their faces with warm, soft Brie and sipping on their drinks.

"It's nice to have you kids along this year," Claire commented to Jack and Emily.

"We wouldn't miss this for the world," Emily said.

That generated another heartfelt hug from Claire, and a playful slap across Jack's head when he offered, "We wanted to see all the old folks at the turn of the century. It may be our last chance."

"Bet us old folks can out-dance you," Joe challenged.

Jack chortled. "Not a prayer," was his cocky response.

After an hour, Joe announced to Claire by his pet name for her, "Time to git Queenie, the dance already started."

"I'll get the car warmed up," Jack said, reaching for his coat. Emily and Claire helped each other don their coats and stood near the doorway waiting for Jack to drive up in the car. Jack opened the passenger door for his Mom and Joe opened Emily's door before riding shotgun.

The ride to the Elks Club was quick, since it was only four miles away. They all exclaimed how cold it was. Joe soon began warning Jack of the dangers of driving on slick wintry roads at night.

"Watch for black ice, kiddo," Joe said.

Jack, polite as ever, responded with a smile, "Thanks, that's good to remember," even though he had heard his dad's warning several hundred times.

The Elks Club was buzzing when they arrived, so it took a few minutes to wind their way through the New Year's Eve revelers to reach their assigned table. Jack and Emily felt out of place. Most of the guests were in their 80s.

Jack felt a long moment of melancholy. He was witnessing the end of a culture. The Elks, Lions, and Jaycee's clubs were the popular spots of the 1950s and 60s. The 70s, 80s and 90s brought new meeting places—discos, bistros, tapas bars, night clubs, and music venues. Wonder what the 2000s will bring?

The band performing that night was popular in the local towns, performing songs from the 1940s, covering Artie Shaw, Glenn Miller, Benny Goodman and all the great bands and singers of that era. Several times during the evening, local crooner "Bernie" sang Bing Crosby, Frank Sinatra, Al Martino, and Mel Tormé tunes. A British guest, Scotty Smythe, joined him on stage. He performed a whimsical song popular during World War II called, "I've Got a Lovely Bunch of Coconuts."

Joe introduced Emily to Scotty and his wife Eva, but Jack missed the meeting because he was at the bar getting their drinks.

Jack and Emily danced the night away. It was almost midnight when they admitted defeat and returned to the table, sweating. Jack's tie and jacket were long discarded; his shirt sleeves were rolled up past his elbows.

"Guess us old folks gotcha beat," Joe chuckled.

"Hate to admit it, but you're right," Jack agreed. Joe gestured to a couple in their 90s that never left the dance floor all evening.

"Build up your aerobics ability so you can compete with those two next New Year's," he said.

At that moment, Bernie stopped crooning a Bing Crosby song to proclaim, "Ladies and Gentlemen, and I use that term loosely, its fifteen seconds to a new century!"

He then launched into the countdown:

"Ten! Nine! Eight! Seven! Six! Five! Four! Three! Two! One— Happy New Year! Happy New Century! Happy 2000!"

Jack gave Emily a long, sweet kiss, savoring the precious moment. Emily smiled to see Joe and Claire kissing each other. The family then shared several moments of hugs, and laughter as they exchanged New Year's greetings.

The band broke out with "Auld Lang Syne," an old Scottish song from the 1700s which means "old long since" or "times gone by."

"We'll drink a cup of kindness yet for times gone by," Bernie crooned.

How appropriate, Jack thought as he surveyed a ballroom full of happy couples who were representative of the generation that preceded him. This is the generation that saved the world with their service in World War II.

Jack knew his dad had served in the Pacific as a Navy medic during the War. "I must ask him someday about his exploits," he mused. "And I'd better do it soon."

The Elks Club gala ended as the older couples filed out, not used to staying out late, even on New Year's Eve. Everyone who passed by their table thanked Jack and Emily for accompanying their parents. They expressed a hint of jealousy. "Wish our kids would come!"

"They'd have a great time here. Tell them how much fun we had!" Emily said.

As the servers started clearing the tables, Joe declared, "I guess the fat lady has sung her last song tonight, gang. Shall we go?" With that, Jack and Joe helped their wives with their coats and walked to the car on the first cold morning of January 2000.

On the ride home, Joe intoned his warnings about black ice and snowdrift perils, plus a new one. "Keep an eye out for all those old people leaving the club who drive as slow as the dickens."

As they pulled into the driveway, Joe invited Jack and Emily in for a nightcap. Jack wanted to say no, but Emily preempted him with, "We'd love to! How often do we get to spend the first morning of a brand-new century together?"

"Only this once, I hope," Claire muttered, "Who wants to live that long?"

They all dashed towards the front door. It was now 2 a.m. and the air was crisp. Jack gazed at the sky teeming with stars. Imitating a famous astronomer, he turned to Emily and announced, "Millions and millions, look at all them stars," only to discover that Emily had rushed into the foyer, muttering behind her through chattering teeth, "That's a great line Jack, but I'm too cold for stargazing.

Jack's entered the kitchen to the sounds of ice clinking against crystal. Joe poured himself his favorite highball, Jack and Ginger: Jack Daniels and ginger ale. Joe offered one to Jack. "Coffee for me, I still have to drive home," he demurred.

As they sat around the kitchen island on barstools talking about the evening, Jack brought up a subject about his Dad that had been bothering him for more than a decade.

After serving in the Navy, Joe worked for a large information technology company, retiring in 1985. For fifteen years since retirement, Joe volunteered about five days a week, providing computer support to schools in the area. He worked countless hours in the school's computer labs, with children from ages eight to eighteen, teaching them about how to use computers at the labs.

Every year, Joe would announce his retirement from his volunteer work, only to have the school superintendent, principals and teachers plead for him to support the schools for another year.

"So, Dad, why do you always go back to working with these school kids?" Jack interjected into the lighthearted conversation between his parents and Emily about the evening's fun. "I know you love to support anyone you can, but you and Mom ought to enjoy your retirement. You ought to be out there traveling, exploring, spending our inheritance."

Jack hated that his Dad received no recognition for his contributions and sacrifices. Jack could count on his mother's support at family gatherings, but this time Claire only said, "Listen to what your father has to say, Jack. He told me today what drives his passion to help children."

Jack turned to his father to see that Joe had tears in his eyes. Jack had never seen his dad cry.

The room was silent, each person unsure of what to say or do next. There was a sudden somber mood in the air.

After a few minutes, Joe spoke. "You may remember I was a Navy medic in the war, But I never told you or your Mom about being behind enemy lines in France as well, because it was such a traumatic experience for me. I was a boy of seventeen when it happened. When I came back, I wanted to put all those horrible nightmares behind me."

"In March 1944, I flew to Scotland in secret and then transported with a team by boat to promote Patton's fake invasion of the Pas-de-Calais. I knew how to build radios blindfolded and I spoke fluent French. My team's mission was to distribute radios to the Free French movement and the Maquis in the field during April and May 1944 and to repair them as needed," Joe continued.

"One night, while I was patrolling the operational area with the French Resistance, I watched in horror as the Nazis hunted and executed a Jewish man and his wife on a narrow, tree-lined lane. Their little daughter saw the whole thing. She ran screaming into the woods, heading straight for me. I tried to calm her, while she fought with every bit of strength in her young body. She looked up at me with tear-filled eyes and said, 'Who will take care of me now? They have butchered my parents.' I told that little girl that my name was Sonny, and that as long as I lived, I'd take care of her," Joe said.

"I didn't know what to do to calm her, so I sang a garbled lullaby that I drew from a song Mom sang to me when I had a fever or something."

Emily and Jack sat in stunned silence as Joe told his story.

"Her name was Charlene. She was eight years old. She felt safe with me. Our team leader took Charlene to the home of a local family for safety and we checked in on her often; taking her toys, books and candy. She was shy and sweet, so she settled in with her new family, and the parents and their three children appeared to love her and make her part of their family unit.

Three weeks later, someone in our camp tipped off the SS about Charlene's identity. Charlene had firsthand knowledge of the partisans' killing of some SS officers.

They broke her leg, her hand, hit her in the head with a gun, and kicked her in the stomach with a military boot. Through all their heinous torture, that brave little girl never ratted on us. Despite the excruciating pain she must have endured, Charlene never said a word.

I could tell no one about the killing and suffering I saw back then, because if I'm still alive, so are those monsters, and I didn't want to expose my family to danger."

Joe's tears continued to flow down his cheek, and he became silent. Claire hugged Joe and ended his painful disclosure. "For another time, Sonny. It's late and the kids have to drive home."

Jack and Emily hugged Joe and Claire longer than usual when saying their goodbyes.

"I still need your help with fixing our bathroom plumbing this weekend," Jack said, hoping to restore the lighthearted mood from earlier.

"Sure," Joe replied, "Call me when you're ready."

Jack and Emily were quiet on the drive home; they sat in the car in their driveway, sobered by what Joe had confessed.

What a frightening experience for a 17-year-old boy to endure, Emily thought.

She turned to Jack; kissed him on the cheek and said, "Isn't it amazing what we never knew about our parents?"

Indeed, thought Jack.

The Armory

It was the summer of 1942. Joe and Raymond were still best buddies. They resided in the adjoining duplexes, attended the same high school, and loved the same hobbies. They resumed practicing Morse code on each other's walls at night, annoying their collective families. Joe still had a crush on Cynthia and Raymond still had a crush on Lois, the same two girls at their high school who remained unapproachable.

In their town, just as in other towns and cities throughout America, the mood was somber. America was still at war with Nazi Germany and Imperial Japan. Most of the town's young men had already gone abroad to fight in the war. When you came back from war duty, you were wounded or in a flag-draped coffin. The only boys around were those too young to serve. Many young boys sought to lie about their age to enlist—impossible to do in a small town.

On a warm summer night, the boys met on the low-hanging roof adjacent to their bedrooms. They discussed girls, baseball, homework, or the latest sci-fi radio show.

Their discussions always led to discourses of the latest battles reported in the news.

They feigned to be generals Dwight Eisenhower and George S. Patton, plotting strategic and tactical decisions to win the war and bring American soldiers back home as national heroes.

Word around school and in town was that representatives of the Army, Navy, Marines, and Coast Guard were coming to the town armory the next day to recruit young men into the armed forces.

The friends had agreed they would attend college; but both Joe and Raymond wanted to fight in the war before they attended university. They plotted about how to persuade their mothers to allow them to enlist at age seventeen. Joe worried that the answer would be an emphatic *no*, since he had received a full scholarship to an Ivy League college just days earlier.

Joe wondered if he could convince his mom about him enlisting for a reserve unit and serving his country while still attending college.

That night, Joe said goodnight to a yawning Raymond. He climbed off the roof and went to bed deep in thought but didn't sleep until near dawn. Even in his state of half-dream, half-awake, Joe couldn't foresee the life-altering event that lurked ahead, ready to catapult him into manhood.

Joe awoke early. He dressed and bounded down the stairs to watch his mother whip up a huge batch of bacon, eggs, coffee, and toast, which he always devoured.

"You're up early, Sonny," Emma said.

"Couldn't sleep mom. Besides, the smell of bacon woke me up," he said, disarming her with a charming grin.

"Mom, I have something to ask you. It's important. You know there's a meeting downtown asking for men to enlist. Before you say no, I want to explain what I'm thinking…"

But Joe didn't get farther. "No, Sonny, I won't let you go off to war! Both of your brothers are leaving for war, and I won't have my youngest child in harm's way, too!"

"But Mom, let me explain. If I join the reserves and go to college, I won't be drafted, but can still wear a uniform. I don't want to be the only guy in town who never got to serve our country."

"I won't hear of it, Sonny! You don't have to prove yourself to be a man in this world; too many young boys and men have already tried and have come home in coffins. I forbid you to go. By and by, when this is over, you will appreciate my decision." Emma said.

Resigned that he could not win this argument, Joe let the matter drop. He plucked at his toast and sipped his coffee, but he was too discouraged to eat his normal breakfast.

To enlist at seventeen, Joe needed his mother's signature, and it was obvious he would not get it. He pondered forging her signature. He reasoned he'd just get snagged. Perhaps he could work at the armory in some other capacity and demonstrate to her he wasn't in harm's way. *Maybe then she'd let me enlist,* Joe thought.

Joe left the dining room and met Raymond outside. Joe's slumped stature and sad eyes spoke volumes. "Your mom said no, too?"

"Yeah, she said I'm too young."

"Me too. Shall we go anyhow?" Raymond invited with that familiar gleam in his eyes.

"Are you nuts? My mom would kill me!"

"I didn't say we should join; I said we should go downtown and see what's up, come on whadaya say?"

"What the heck," Joe said, knowing better than to argue, "Let's go."

It was early June 1942, but the two boys ran the five miles to the armory, undeterred by summer's early heat and muggy air. Joe and Raymond slowed to a walk when they were in front of the drugstore. They stared at a long line of men outside the armory, many of who looked too young or too old to serve. The best shot for 4-F men was to get into a state guard unit.

Joe and Raymond were gripped with panic. They had heard that the Army was recruiting for the state guard unit, but the line was already so long.

"The recruiting quota will be met before we ever get to the front of the line," Joe griped under his breath.

At the armory, starched white tablecloths covered rickety tables arranged in an L-shape, set up with brochures about serving in the Army, Navy, Marines, and Coast Guard.

Raymond chuckled when he saw the Coast Guard table.

"Look, Joe, it's the Shallow Water Navy! Do you know why all the Coast Guard recruits are six feet tall? So when their boat sinks, they can walk back to shore!"

Joe whacked him on the head. "Shut up, Raymond! If it weren't for the Coast Guard, the Nazis would live at your house!"

As the boys entered, a guardsman by the name of "Old Jacob," a World War I veteran, intercepted them at the door.

"Do your mothers know you're here, boys?"

"They know. We're just here to get some brochures and see the guys in uniform," Joe lied with a grin.

"Best behave or I'll run you both out with yer britches stinging!" Old Jacob admonished.

"Yesss sirrr," the boys saluted Old Jacob, getting a snort from the veteran.

During their rooftop rendezvous at night, Joe and Raymond often plotted that they would fake their age and get into the service as many others had done. However, Joe knew that if he did, his two brothers— Clarence, who was joining the Merchant Marine, and Armand, who enlisted in the Navy—would take leave just to come beat him senseless. *Besides Armand and Clarence, I'd have to deal with Mom's wrath, since many of her best friends had lost their sons already*, Joe thought.

There were two sights that were most dreaded in town during 1942. The first was U.S. cargo planes landing at the local airport, unloading the bodies of young men in coffins draped in red, white, and blue flags. The second was the Western Union man, riding down the street on his bicycle, delivering telegrams to resident families. You held your breath, frozen in time, from the moment you saw him until he passed your house; then you were relieved.

Joe's brothers were adamant that he stayed home to take care of their Mom, just in case the Western Union courier knocked on their front door.

It jolted Joe back to reality when a disabled Marine captain with flaming red hair turned towards the audience in a wheelchair to begin his address. The makeshift podium at which he sat was brought in from a nearby church, cut to about three feet so his notes were within arm's reach.

The crowd stirred in excitement as Sam Carlson, Commander of the State Guard unit, surveyed the young men gathered. A West Point graduate, Carlson was from their hometown, four years ahead of Joe and Raymond in high school.

Newspapers throughout America reported Captain Carlson's heroic actions. When Japanese forces encircled his company one night, Captain Carlson grabbed a bag of hand grenades and ran in a circle, throwing them at the enemy. Carlson saved his men and earned the Navy Cross for gallantry. But he suffered a career-ending leg injury. Still eager to serve his country, he volunteered to lead the state's guard unit.

Just prior to speaking to the audience, he flashed back to that battle on Guadalcanal. Bullets whizzed over Captain Carlson's head. He dove headfirst into the nearest foxhole with his radioman, Corporal Teddy Mack. Carlson had been expecting the enemy attack which he knew would come tonight. He prepared his company of Marines. He pulled back the bolt on his Thompson submachine gun, nicknamed the Chicago Typewriter.

He aimed the weapon down the hill towards the dense jungle.

Come on you bastards, he thought, what are you waiting for!

Months earlier, in August 1942, Captain Samuel "Red"

Carlson's Easy Company landed on the island of Guadalcanal. Captain Carlson was with the 5th Marine Regiment, 1st Marine Division under Major General Vandegrift, on Guadalcanal, in the southern Solomon Islands.

The operation was to be a quick one, so most of his men only had bolt action 1903 Springfield rifles and a meager ten-day supply of ammunition. They designated the assault on the island "Operation Shoestring."

When the Marines landed, they overwhelmed the six hundred Imperial Japanese soldiers who occupied the island since May of that year. The Japanese would not give up so easily, reinforcing the island to retake the vital Henderson Airfield.

Captain Carlson received orders to position his company on top of Lunga Ridge. The ridge offered a natural avenue of approach to the airfield and commanded the surrounding area. His company dug in at a clearing on top. It offered a natural defensive position, with 360-degree views of the jungle below them.

Easy Company cleared out lanes of fire for the M2 Browning .50 caliber machine gun team and two teams with M1919 Browning .30 caliber machine guns, before the enemy started attacking his defensive position. When the attacks came as expected, the charging Japanese troops were like cattle to the slaughter.

Since Lunga Ridge was high ground, and the enemy knew well of its tactical significance. Because of that, most of the attacks were directed at Captain Carlson's Easy Company holding the high ground.

***

October 24th, 2300 hours: Captain Carlson was looking for his radioman, Corporal Teddy Mack. Carlson reflected on the previous night, when elements of Maruyama's division of the

Japanese Imperial Army had attacked their position. Carlson's company and the other companies on the defensive line had pushed the Japs back into the jungle. Tonight, Easy Company expected another frontal assault by the determined Japanese to break the line and recapture Henderson Airfield.

Carlson jumped in a foxhole next to his radioman, Corporal Teddy Mack, hunkered down eating his K-ration. The heat was overwhelming; the sweat stained his uniform. He smelled bad, but so did everyone else.

The sounds of the jungle beasts continued non-stop. It reminded the captain of the crickets back home. But these were much more dangerous than mere crickets. The sounds of the jungle; bugs and monkey sounds filled the air in the distance. He had lost a man a few nights back to a jaguar. Because of that loss, he ordered that no one go into the jungle alone.

"Still quiet out there, cap?" Mack asked.

"Except for them damn monkeys!" Carlson replied. "The Japs will try another assault soon."

If the Marines heard the sounds of the jungle from their foxholes, they knew that they could let their guards down.

When it got quiet, all the Marines stiffened their grips on their weapons, straining to see any movement of Japanese troops approaching from the jungle, trying to sneak up on them. As the noises returned, they visibly relaxed and slid back down into their foxholes.

"The battery on the radio is almost dead, we're gonna need to send a runner back to get another battery at the airfield from battalion," Corporal Mack said.

"Have you been able to contact anyone at battalion?" The captain said.

"No sir, I'm just getting static," Corporal Mack said.

"I would rather have them send someone up to deliver those batteries, I can't afford to lose any more men," the captain said, picking up his Thompson submachine gun. "Keep trying, I'm headed over to check on 1st Platoon."

Easy Company maintained at seventy-five percent strength by the division. Carlson's commanders kept his company gave Easy Company priority on reinforcements to hold the ridge. Major air and sea battles had previously taken place. Each side vied for control of the sea and airspace above the island. Whoever won those battles would control the island. Carlson watched those battles from his foxhole, cheering on the Marine Wildcat air squadrons as they sparred with the Japanese Zeros in a deadly dance in the skies above them.

Even though reinforcements arrived daily, the psychological toll on the Marines affected their ability to take the fight to the enemy. The Japs mounted suicidal banzai attacks on the defensive position. Night after night they attacked, throwing their battle-hardened imperial troops into the Marines, trying to break them. After each attack, mornings light revealed the hillside covered in dead Japanese soldiers, some stacked two to four high as Easy Company cut them down by the machine gun teams as they tried to climb over fallen comrades.

To Carlson, it seemed as if they didn't value life; instead, dying in useless attacks on their strong defensive positions. Carlson had requested that his company rotate from the front lines on a more frequent basis, but they denied him. Everything available man rotated into the front lines to defend the vital airfield. General Vandegrift had ordered that the Marines hold the defensive positions at all costs until reinforcements arrived, if they would at all.

October 25th, 0300 hours: Captain Carlson moved to the center of his company's defensive position when all hell broke loose. Mortar rounds burst all around their defensive position, followed by crazed Japanese soldiers charging out of the jungle with bayonets fixed in a banzai charge. They raced towards the

American defensive lines screaming at the top of their lungs, bent on killing every living thing in sight. The battle-hardened Marines donned helmets and charged their weapons to repel the enemy. Marines cut down wave after wave of attacking Japanese, but their lines weakened by the mounting casualties. Already two of his positions to his left flank had been overrun; Marines were bayoneted as they tried to push the enemy from their foxholes. Carlson pulled his reserve platoon from the rear of his lines and led them towards the collapsing left flank. He sprayed bullets from his Thompson submachine gun, cutting down several enemy soldiers. The reserve platoon took back the left flank, driving the enemy back down the hill onto the open-fire lanes of Easy Company's machine guns. The rat-tat-tat of the Browning machine guns sliced into the enemy, leaving none standing.

Platoon Sergeant Williams commanded the left flank of the defensive position. He directed the fire from their Browning .30 caliber machine gun.

"Sarge, they're everywhere," the private manning the machine gun yelled.

"Concentrate on the largest mass of troops!" the sergeant directed, firing his M1 Garand at an approaching enemy with his bayonet fixed. He dropped the Jap with a bullet to the chest.

"Everyone else watch your lanes!" he shouted over the din of battle.

A mortar round exploded with a deafening crash a few yards in front of the machine gun nest's position, stunning the crew and Sergeant Williams. When the smoke and dust cleared from the near fatal explosion, the enemy confronted them. The sergeant fought back, knowing the Japs would give no quarter. He fired point blank into the enemy, aiming and killing as if he were in a shooting gallery.

The men manning the machine gun fell back as several Japanese soldiers crested the berm of the foxhole. The enemy soldiers bayoneted the crew, killing them. Sergeant Williams fired into the concentrated enemy until he heard the dreaded sound of his empty ammunition clip clang as it exited the M1 Garand. To his relief he had cleared the foxhole of the Japs.

He scanned the area when he realized that Captain Carlson had led a squad of men to his position. The captain and the squad drove the Jap soldiers back, killing every enemy near the sergeant's foxhole. The sergeant waved to his commander that he was all right, when a strange thud hit the ground in his foxhole. Looking down, he saw a grenade lying by his feet. He started to scramble out the back of the foxhole, but he didn't make it. The grenade exploded, killing him.

Captain Carlson halted, diving into a nearby foxhole. He adjusted his helmet to see if the sergeant had made it. The mangled corpse of Sergeant Williams lay half out of the foxhole. He pounded his fist on the ground in frustration and anger. The firing had stopped. The enemy had faded back into the jungle once again.

Standing up, he slung the Thompson over his shoulder, not looking at the sergeant, but focused his attention to the jungle.

"Get Doc up here," Carlson said to the Marine in his foxhole. "Tell him to bring something to cover him up."

The grenade that exploded on that position destroyed the machine gun beyond repair. Equipment was scarce and losing a vital piece of the defense would have dire consequences. Easy Company was down to two machine gun teams. Carlson went to his command position, occupied by one of his men.

"Private," he said, "Get back to battalion at Henderson. Tell them we need another machine gun, with a crew. If they don't have that, a mortar or anything that fires more than these damn Springfields and Garands.

"Yes sir!" the private said. He turned on a heel and disappeared into the jungle.

Damn, the captain thought. *I don't even know that kid's name.*

The latest attack was only a probe, to find out and exploit the weakest part of Easy Company's line. The captain expected a much larger force to follow.

Captain Carlson went back to his foxhole. Corporal Mack sat in the foxhole, cleaning off his rifle.

"Mack, get me battalion on the line," Captain Carlson said. "Let's see if we can get some support from those arty bastards for once."

"Roger," Mack replied. He turned on the radio and spoke into the microphone.

After a few minutes of back and forth, Carlson was assigned a dedicated battery of artillery for their defense.

"Let's hope it's enough to keep the Japs off our backs." Carlson said.

October 25th, 2200 hours: Throughout the night, supported by artillery, Easy Company defeated wave after wave of frontal Japanese attacks, including hand-to-hand fighting. Just when they thought the enemy would overrun them; Corporal Mack would call in an artillery strike that would clear the field of the enemy. Even with the support, Easy Company still lost men. Several of Captain Carlson's men became walking wounded. Even though they should have evacuated to the rear, they refused to leave. None of the wounded Marines wanted to leave their buddies. Carlson positioned those men to the rear with the duty of ammunition resupply and to assist the company medic.

October 26th, 2200 hours: The Japanese attack began just after nightfall, when Carlson's company came under an immediate and fierce hail of bullets. They came in, wave after wave, Carlson's machine guns mowing them all down. His remaining .30 caliber machine gun overheated and refused to fire again. A bullet had pierced the water-cooled sleeve surrounding the barrel. Without the suppressive fire of the machine gun, the Japanese overran that strongpoint, bayoneting the two men inside. Captain Carlson led his reserves against this new threat, pushing the enemy back over the hill. Shouting out orders to his remaining .50 caliber team, he had them move into his foxhole to cover the depleted company from the center. It would have to do. He spread out his remaining Marines in pairs to cover the entire front. He was now down to a fifty percent effective fighting force. He went to the positions that had been overrun and helped the men around him remove the bodies of their fallen fellow Marines.

A second wave of Japanese approached the remaining .50 caliber machine gun team in the center position. Calling out to 3rd Platoon, entrenched on the right flank, he had them give up one man in each foxhole to double up in the manpower in the center of the line to face this new enemy attack. His reserves now gone, Easy Company's defensive position to the rear was wide open; the exception being of his walking wounded. Easy Company was running out of men.

"Teddy, get battalion on the line," the captain ordered. "Tell HQ to get us those reserves, tell them we have at least two battalions attacking our position."

"Yes, sir," Sergeant Mack said. With a flick, he turned on the radio. It had a low charge, but he could get battalion on the line. After explaining the ensuing firefight, he could get the reserves released.

Two more waves of Japanese assaulted the .50 caliber machine gun position. If they succeeded, Carlson knew they would be over run and the enemy would recapture Henderson Airfield. But Carlson's timely placement of 3rd Platoon into the center of the line enabled the Marines to fend off the attackers.

As Carlson's company fired down at the approaching Japanese, the walking wounded in the rear came under attack by several Japanese carrying Type 99 short rifles with bayonets fixed. They had flanked and infiltrated his weakened defense. Jumping up from his foxhole, he shouted out orders to the 2nd Platoon's Sergeant Denison to follow him in to repel the Japs, now involved with the wounded Marines in the rear. It was a slaughter. The American wounded had no chance.

Not stopping to wait for 2nd Platoon, Captain Carlson ran up to one Jap soldier in a foxhole, firing point blank into his chest, throwing him back. He was dead before he hit the ground. Before Carlson could react, a second Jap appeared above him on the crest of the foxhole and stabbed him in the leg with his bayonet, and pulled it out, pulling the trigger. Captain Carlson heard an audible click. He didn't hesitate and clubbed his attacker in the head with the butt of his machine gun, knocking him unconscious. He then swung the Thompson down and fired a short burst into the hated enemy.

The 2nd Platoon came up behind their commander. Maneuvering to the rear they forced the remaining Jap's back with a hail of bullets.

Defeated, the remaining Japanese blended back into the jungle. They could hear the screams of their dead in the dense darkness beyond. Captain Carlson took stock of his wound as he collapsed in the foxhole, next to the Jap's he had just killed. The bayonet had cut him deep.

"Shit!" he shouted, pulling a dirty scarf from his pocket to stop the bleeding. "Damn Japs!"

Sergeant Denison, seeing the captain lying in the foxhole, holding onto his mangled leg, yelled for the company's medic, Sergeant Waldron. The medic ran over and bandaged up the wound the best he could.

"We need to get you to the battalion's aid station, Cap," The medic said.

"Just get me bandaged up and back in my foxhole," Carlson said. "I am not leaving my command post with the Japs out there."

"Sir, you're lucky his gun jammed," Sergeant Denison said.

"Either his gun jammed, or they ordered him not to load his rifle for the sneak attack, my lucky day," the captain said.

Sergeant Denison picked up one of the Jap's rifles and pulled out the magazine clip from underneath. "Empty," he said. "I guess you're right, Cap. These guys were on a suicide mission."

Finishing up his bandage, the medic helped the captain to his feet. Carlson took the Jap rifle from Sergeant Denison and tried to use it as a crutch. He made it three steps before he crumbled to the ground.

"Sergeant Denison, can you get one of your men to help me with the captain? We need to get him out of here," the medic said. "Looks like you're going home, sir."

***

Sam Carlson began speaking in a tone that was sincere.

"Our Armed Forces welcome you to the Armory. That you and other young Americans will fight against the tyranny and oppression of the Germans and Japanese should prove to all that there are men throughout America still ready, able, and willing to carry on this great fight for freedom."

Captain Carlson expressed his hope that at war's end, all nations could live in peace, not conflict. He bemoaned how fragile life was; how tragic that all across America, small towns are bereft of their young men. He lamented at how many stars adorned the front windows of American homes, symbolizing the ultimate sacrifice of American families. He asked for a moment of silence to honor all those who gave their lives in service. Captain Carlson concluded his address with words that touched Joe and Raymond.

"We are hurting as a community and a country, but we are not alone. Please remember that in every country across the globe, families are mourning their own lost ones. I pray every day that we can end this conflict soon, so that our families can reunite, and rebuild their lives.

"War is cruel. But it can unite people from all countries, races and religions. I declare that our American young men will make lifelong friends from the Allied team members they serve in this war, whether from England, France, Canada, and Poland."

After Captain Carlson's address, Joe and Raymond approached the table, seeking pamphlets and posters from each service to add to their collections. It delighted them to receive recruitment forms with urging to join and serve their country. Joe and Raymond were very keen on the Army, since both had shot rifles since they were kids, hunting the local woods together. To them, the Army's mission seemed a good fit.

I wouldn't mind serving in the Navy either, since I love boats and ships, Joe thought.

Joe and Raymond collected several pamphlets but no posters for their bedrooms. Disappointed, they prepared to leave. Just then, Captain Carlson waved them over.

"Boys, err, I mean, *men*," Carlson stammered, "You know, if you wanted to help around the armory on weekends during the school year and full time during the summer, we could use your help around here cleaning weapons, stocking shelves, and mowing the grounds. We are short on men to maintain the place, with the war and all."

In unison, both Joe and Raymond yelled out "Sure!" Joe backpedaled, adding, "With Mom's permission."

"I'm sure you boys could use some pin money, so I'll bring this up with your parents at church on Sunday," Captain Carlson promised.

"That'd be great," Raymond acknowledged. Turning to Joe, he bragged: "We're in like Flynn, kid!"

The boys left the armory with a lot more bounce to their step than when they arrived and had faced a long line of applicants.

Saluting "Old Jacob" as they marched military style out of the Armory front door and down the cracked and crumbling cement steps to the sidewalk below, they teased: "Hey Jacob, when ya gonna fix 'em steps?"

The fall of 1942, and most of 1943 went by in a blur for Joe. He was a regular fixture at the armory and had joined the State Guard.

Joe spoke fluent French, thanks to speaking French and English in his household while growing up. His mother, Emma, a French Canadian from Nova Scotia, immigrated to the United States when she was twenty-three.

When his State Guard buddies ribbed Joe about how France fell to the Nazis in World War II, Joe felt compelled to point out his mother was French Canadian, not French.

For Sonny and Raymond, it replaced their carefree and innocent days with somber nights of stoic patriotism and heightened national pride. In homes and in taverns across America, there were victorious shouts and tears for every drop of positive news about the Allied effort.

Joe was impatient for active duty. He wanted to serve his country in the real fight with the enemy. Most of his fellow guardsmen were too young to join active duty, just like old men, 4-Fs, and those who were wounded and unable to reenlist. Carlson and Joe had collaborated on building radios as a hobby, so it was natural that Carlson made Joe his radioman during field exercises. Captain Carlson walked with a pronounced limp, but he never complained, and Joe took care not to mention his injury.

In the spring of 1944, rumors flew about an impending allied invasion of Europe. Most people in their town bet it would take place in the Southern part of France, where allied troops, with a large contingent of American soldiers, had made steady progress from North Africa through Sicily to Italy.

Conflicting news circulated on an almost daily basis that ships with Canadian and American troops were sailing daily to England, giving serious rise to doubt of a Southern invasion. The Germans, no doubt, would be prepared.

"It's gonna get worse for our boys before it gets better," Captain Carlson predicted.

On March 12, 1944, Captain Sam Carlson approached Joe with a request for active duty that would redefine his life.

So Many Questions

On July 5, 2000, the day of his father's seventy-third birthday, after a fun Fourth of July celebration, Jack lost his job. After spending two weeks in denial, Jack began sending off resumes via email, snail mail, and through headhunters. He followed up with many calls. He went on five first interviews and had three follow-up interviews but received no offers.

Emily's job provided enough for both of them to get by. Despite his disappointment at not finding a job at once, Jack savored his newfound freedom, spending countless hours in the garden and doing maintenance around the house.

This isn't so bad, he thought. *I could get used to this, but Emily shouldn't carry financial burden of our expenses by herself.*

Fine job, he thought, surveying his manicured lawn and trimmed hedges. He loved the smell of cut grass. He wiped the dirt and grass stains from his hands.

If I were younger, I might do this for a living.

So far this spring and summer he had planted a row of heather lining the driveway, dwarf Alberta Spruce along the 180 feet of fence line, a multitude of perennials ranging from roses, iris, peonies, and day lilies to clematis, and columbine, plus anything else Emily found at the local farm and garden center on her way home from work.

Every evening, when Emily opened the car door in their driveway, Jack prepared for the first words out of her mouth: "I brought you something!" to which Jack replied, half teasing: "Great! More work!"

"Wouldn't want you to get bored," Emily said, kissing him. He chased her around the yard with a garden hose. That ritual made her squeal and run into the house for cover.

Now mid-July, over seven months after his father's tearful confessions from his stint in World War II, Jack had not dared approach the topic again.

Nagging questions consumed Jack.

I can only guess what happened to Dad in that war. But only he can fill in the blanks, Jack thought.

But he wanted his father to be the first to reintroduce a memory that distressed him. *I'm sure there's so much more to Dad's story*, Jack thought.

Up to this point in his life, Jack had learned that his dad served as a Navy medic in the Pacific, saving countless lives. From what he said on New Year's Day, he served behind enemy lines in France before his service with the Navy in the Pacific.

On July 28, 2000, Emily and Jack visited their local animal shelter and adopted Sassy, a German shepherd mix. *My dad has always had a fierce distrust of Germans*, Jack thought, scratching Sassy's head as he signed the adoption papers. *But when he meets you Labor Day weekend, I'm sure he'll love you, Sassy, even if you have German ancestry.*

During his 329 days of unemployment, Jack adopted a routine that kept him busy and satisfied. He awoke at 6 a.m. to brew a fresh pot of Emily's favorite Costa Rican coffee, and made her eggs, bacon, and toast before she left for work at 7:30 a.m.

After she left, Jack went to his basement office, responded to Help Wanted ads, and emailed resumes and cover letters. By 11 a.m., he was in the garden and yard, removing weeds, trimming, planting, and deadheading rose bushes. Sassy followed him everywhere.

"It's getting hot out here, Sassy. Let's take a break," Jack said. Sassy didn't argue; she was eager to greet her oversized stainless-steel water bowl. Jack picked up the rake and shovel he had laid on the ground and returned both to the shed. Sassy played scout, leading him towards the back door to the house, panting.

From 2 to 4 p.m. each weekday, Jack took a break from the high-ninety-degree temperatures and oppressive humidity. When they entered the house, Jack flipped on the air conditioner in the window and drew the shades closed, as he did every day.

He filled a glass of iced tea from the pitcher in the refrigerator and headed for his basement office, where the temperature was akin to a good wine cellar. Sassy draped her body on the cool cement.

Most afternoons, Jack checked email, called headhunters and paid bills. But this afternoon, he was on an information hunt. At his computer, Jack started a search for World War II covert operations to help him learn more of his dad's experience.

Jack's research hit pay dirt. He learned of Operation Skye, and of Operations Fortitude that created fake radio traffic in a wider deception plan designed to conceal the Allied plan to invade Normandy (Operation Overlord). Radio operators would pass fake radio messages among themselves, mimicking the radio traffic the real unit would generate, hoping that the enemy would intercept the transmissions. Jack read on about fake football scores and even wedding announcements for nonexistent troops."

This must be what Dad was involved with, Jack thought, but he could not find any mention of his father's name. *Did he use a code name? I ought to ask Dad; but when? And how do I ask questions?*

Browsing through news and local events websites, Jack's interest was piqued by an event scheduled for August 8th. A speaker was coming into town with a talk called "Operation Overlord: The Invasion of Europe." Of special note to Jack was that the speaking engagement was at the Elks Club, where their family had attended the New Year's Eve dance.

Interesting, Jack thought, *now I can at least ask someone questions and have a chance of getting the answers to fill in the blanks related to my dad's role behind enemy lines.* Jack removed his credit card from his wallet to pay the fifteen-dollar ticket fee. *Dad may want to go*, he thought, purchasing two tickets.

He called his dad, letting him know he purchased tickets for the presentation. Joe was interested and agreed to go.

"Pick me up fifteen minutes prior," Joe said.

Jack jumped into his 1998 Dodge Durango. The SUV's passenger door popped open on its own while he was driving. Jack kept procrastinating on fixing the troublesome door. He hoped for a new truck.

Emily's reply, "It's cheaper to get it fixed. When you're employed again, we can buy a new car or truck."

As a temporary fix, Jack used a small piece of rope to secure the front passenger door to the back door, holding it in place through the armrest. *It is time I got that damn door fixed*, Jack thought.

Jack pulled into his parents' driveway. His dad waited for him by the house.

"I see your passenger door is still kaput," he said.

Jack grimaced. "I'll take it to the body shop tomorrow."

"Need some money?" Joe asked.

"No, but thanks anyhow," Jack replied.

Joe waited for Jack to remove the rope holding the door. He climbed in the front seat and secured the rope.

When they arrived at the Elks club, Joe and Jack noticed a smattering of what appeared to be World War II veterans and their grown children seated auditorium style near the front.

They walked in and handed their tickets to an older woman wearing an Elks Club shirt and a baseball cap.

"Fill in the rows from the front," she said.

Joe and Jack took their seats. Joe tapped on the shoulder of a man in front of him.

"How ya doin', Eddie?" he asked.

"Hey Joe, nice to see you again! Did you come for a history lesson?" Eddie asked.

"Ha," replied Joe, "Don't care if I *never* remember a minute."

"Jack, Eddie was a Navy Medic. He went into a cave on Iwo and pulled two Marines out. He got a Bronze Star for that one," Joe said.

"Yeah, I came back with a bronze medal, a bunch of heavier metal in my left knee, and a permanent limp," Eddie shot back.

"I can't imagine how grateful those two Marines are to be alive today, thanks to your bravery," Jack said.

"Yeah, I guess," Eddie mumbled.

As the town clock chimed 1 p.m., the speaker walked out onto the club's old stage. The crowd whispered in surprise. They had expected a grizzled old male warrior, not a thirtysomething, tall, blonde woman. Her long hair was pulled back in a chignon and she wore a figure-hugging lavender suit with a white blouse and stiletto black high heels, making her slender legs appear even longer.

Her name was Gisele Toffler. She said she was born in Germany and that her mother's father, Frederik Gustav, worked for the German postal service during World War II.

She explained that she was touring America to tell the story of how her grandfather contributed to the invasion of Normandy and the allied cause by working as a double agent for the allied forces. As she described Operation Fortitude and its sub operations, it mesmerized Jack. He sat upright, bursting with questions. His dad appeared restless in his seat as he listened to Gisele's commentaries.

These hard chairs are tough on Dad's back, Jack supposed.

Gisele concluded her talk after two hours and then fielded questions from the audience, but Jack didn't ask any of his burning questions.

I need to talk with her in person after the presentation, he thought.

Joe was eager to leave during the question-and-answer session, saying Claire needed him to do a chore for her at home. But Jack was adamant, wanting to talk further with Gisele. He asked his dad to stay seated for a few minutes longer and walked up to the stage.

Gisele packed her laptop into her briefcase, speaking with two other guests. Jack introduced himself when the two older gentlemen left the stage.

"Your talk fascinated me, Gisele, and I would love to hear more. They deployed my dad in Europe during the time frame you discussed but he doesn't talk much about it. Maybe if you are in town for a while, my wife and I could take you out to dinner?"

"My next speaking engagement is in a few days. I am some time, until then. Here's my card, call me and we shall see," Gisele said.

"I look forward to a meeting soon," Jack said.

Joe was chatting with old friends about state politics and the weather.

"What did she say?" Joe asked.

"Nothing much. I just wanted to say thanks for the talk," Jack said.

He didn't mention inviting Gisele to dinner. Jack wanted to learn what his dad had been involved with during World War II.

Hell, Dad's war experiences happened fifty-six years ago, Jack thought. *Why is Dad still so paranoid? Whoever they are, they have long forgotten about Allied soldiers like him.*

Jack called Emily, and his account of the blonde female German speaker whose grandfather was a double agent piqued her interest in going out to dinner.

"Jealousy got you to go along, didn't it?" Jack teased Emily.

"No, it's been a rough day at work, so I thank you for saving me from wondering what to prepare for supper tonight," Emily said, laughing. "Let's plan for 7 p.m. at our regular spot?"

Jack called Gisele, who answered her phone on the first ring. She was excited to be going to The High Tide, a favorite restaurant among locals. Jack gave her the address, and they agreed to meet there at 7 p.m.

Good, thought Jack, *maybe now I can get answers.*

My English Vacation

At about 3 p.m. on March 12, 1944, as Joe was completing the assembly of two radios at the armory, he recognized Captain Carlson walking towards him, leaning on his cane.

The damp spring air must make his pain worse, Joe thought.

Captain Carlson asked Sonny to follow him to his office at the back of the armory. When they were both seated, Carlson said, "The Brits are looking for radio operators for an upcoming covert operation. If you're interested, you'll ship out to Scotland, where you'll help with radio communications to support partisans in France. I thought of you when this unusual request came in, since you speak fluent French and you know radio electronics like the back of your hand."

"Wow, sure!" Joe replied. *How will I tell Mom?* Joe thought with some trepidation. He had been so morose about missing out on war action. Now that the opportunity was forthcoming, it all seemed to be happening all too fast.

"You can't tell anyone about this, Joe," the captain warned. "This is a top-secret mission and requires utmost discretion on your part. If you go, the official word will be that you're being deployed for duty in another state for a few months."

Joe knew that this was not unusual.

"Your deployment will be on or about April 4th, and they will require you till about June 15th," Captain Carlson said. "Other than that, I have very little information. Here is whom you are to contact for travel to Scotland."

He handed Joe a folder stamped *Top Secret* on the cover.

"When you arrive in Scotland, a member of MI6 Secret Intelligence Service named Major Scotty Smythe will contact you. MI6 is a top-notch unit. You'll be in great hands, Joe."

"I deploy in less than three weeks; not much time to get ready," Joe commented, a little nervous.

I do not understand what I have to get ready for, he thought.

"Will I be going by ship?" he asked.

"No, you'll take a B-24 from New Hampshire through Canada to Iceland for refueling, and then on to Scotland. Start your preparations, Joe, and pack light. You'll be outfitted once you arrive in Scotland."

The weeks until Joe's departure passed. Mom had asked the usual questions about when he would return. But she appeared comfortable with her Sonny's explanation about a State Guard assignment in Iowa, much to Joe's relief. He was nervous and excited at the same time and hoped he would not fail on such an important secret mission.

At a small airport in New Hampshire at dawn on April 2, Joe boarded the B-24 bomber named Sugar Baby. He climbed up through the belly of the bomber and met Radioman John Matus, who was about 5 years older than Joe.

"Strap in, kid; it's gonna be a long, bumpy flight."

That's when it struck Joe: *he was going to war*.

Radioman Matus' log read:

Log;

Left Langley Field, May 2, 1944. Arrived at Grenier Field in New Hampshire the same day. Picked up a passenger, a young kid named Joe on his way to Scotland. Flew over Quebec in Canada, landed in Labrador, spent forty-eight hours there. Took off from Labrador and landed in Iceland, spent the night there. Took off flying over Greenland, a cold barren looking place. Observed a glacier...Landed in Prestwick, Scotland, dropped off passenger Joe to some British officer named William Fowlie Smythe.

Sent to Stone, England; remained there one week and then established in the 446 Bomb Group, 704 Bomb Sq., Bungay, England; near Dover on the wash.

The flight across the Atlantic was bumpy but uneventful, offset by a lengthy refueling stop in Iceland and a tricky landing in a dense fog at Prestwick, Scotland. The pilot, Griff, bounced the plane off the runway three times before touching down on the wet runway.

"I guess Griff can log this in as three landings," John said, winking at Joe. Joe could only manage a weak smile; his stomach churned from the bumpy landing. He couldn't see anything through the fog.

Joe stepped off the ladder and onto the runway. He did not understand where he was, the thick fog making the whole scene surreal and mysterious. It was like the farewell scene from *Casablanca*; he half expected to see Humphrey Bogart emerging through the darkness.

"Salutations, Joe!" he heard a British accent call out. "My name is Major Scotty Smythe, which is all you must know for now. We will travel a few hours distance from here by a truck."

"Nice to meet you sir," Sonny said.

"Damn this bloody fog," cursed Major Smythe, making no effort to hide his disdain for the poor weather. "You can freshen up in the OPS center before we go. We leave in 20 minutes."

"Where are we headed, Major?" Joe asked.

"That's not for discussion here," the major replied before marching away. "Come along then."

After using the "loo" and getting a cup of tea from the operations center, the major appeared in the doorway and announced that their transport had arrived. It was a British troop truck, and as the flap opened, Joe observed five other men in civilian clothes lining the side benches. He hopped in and nodded to the others. No one spoke during the ride. From time to time, someone grunted when the truck hit a pothole.

The rest of that foggy cold night was a blur. Two British soldiers carrying Sten guns outfitted in battle gear escorted Joe into a barracks. On his bed were some tan pants and shirts, a pair of boots, several pairs of brown socks, undergarments, a black beret, and a sealed envelope.

One soldier commented, "The major suggests that you get some rest, mate. The loo is just outside to your left if the need should arise. Briefing is outside at 5 a.m. sharp."

Joe picked up a sealed envelope. It contained just one word on a plain white sheet of paper: *Sonny.*

No sooner than Sonny felt his head hit the pillow, he heard a voice whisper in his ear, "Welcome, time to get up."

"I'm up! I'm up! What's going on?" he protested.

"Well, young man, what's *going on*," Major Smythe said imitating Sonny, "is that you responded in English and if this was not an exercise, you'd be dead."

"If I was Jerry, you'd have a bullet in the head or be well on your way to a concentration camp by now," admonished Major Smythe. "Learn to speak French every waking moment and in your sleep, if you want to live to a ripe old age."

Sonny sensed the ominous warning in Smythe's voice.

Why do I have to speak French when I'm in Scotland for God's sake, Sonny wondered? *Is there something more to the mission that they haven't told me about yet?*

"Now, get some rest. Formation will be outside at 5 a.m. sharp." With that, the major left the barracks.

Sonny's eyes were still open when the major entered the barracks shouting, "Rise and shine, mates! Step outside for the morning brief."

During the night, Sonny had dressed in his new uniform, but couldn't find his watch and wallet. Both had disappeared. He thought maybe a thief had taken them during the night but wasn't sure.

Must have dropped them in the truck, Sonny thought, *I must ask the major.*

Outside they lined up, Dress Right Dress, Sonny fitting in as he did many times before in the Guard drills. When they had all lined up, the major spoke in an almost gentle tone.

"Welcome to our little paradise, lady and gentlemen," nodding to the men before turning to a slim, petite dark-haired woman, with green eyes and curly hair cut short in a fetching bob, who stood at attention at the end of the line.

Sonny glanced in surprise at the beautiful woman.

She looks French, he thought.

"Something wrong?" Major Smythe asked.

"No, Sir," he replied, which caused the French woman to roll her eyes.

The major sighed; "Right, stand at ease, *men,*" he said.

"Welcome to MI6. You have all volunteered for this mission. I will brief each of you individually. I have assigned you code names, associated with your past, which you found on your bunks this morning. We have also removed any personal items to keep your identity secret. You must never identify yourselves by your real name to each other or to anyone else during this top-secret mission. If you do so, you will find yourself shipped back straightaway to the unit that sent you to me."

"It is very unwise to give your real name in this business because double agents abound everywhere. One of you may, in fact, be one," the major intoned. "It is likewise unwise to trust anyone; I repeat, *anyone.*"

The major spoke for about twenty minutes about protocol regarding saluting, the boundaries of their camp, mealtimes and mess hall protocol, and formation times. Sonny's thoughts wandered to the French girl in line while the major droned on.

It startled him out of his daydream when the major said in his ear: "I said *dismissed,* Sonny."

As he turned, he stumbled into the French girl, saying in French, "*Pardon.*"

She smiled and replied in French, "*C'est bon*, what's your code name?"

"Sonny."

"You have a different accent. Are you from Canada?"

"*Oui*, my mother's from Nova Scotia and immigrated to America," he said.

"Your French-Canadian accent is a problem! Perhaps we can practice the true dialect together," the woman said with a wink.

"That would be great," Sonny replied. "What's *your* code name?"

"Marie," she replied, "I have many code names, but Marie is my favorite."

Joining Sonny and Marie in this mission were two British agents with code names Cameron and Horace, and a Spaniard with the code name Sergio. Cameron and Horace spoke French with a British accent. Sergio, who had dark black hair and yellow cat eyes, spoke French, English, and Spanish. He appeared shy and seldom spoke to the others.

The days went by. On day two, Major Smythe reminded the agents that they only speak in French. The team trained with an introduction to British wireless, how to take radios apart, repair and rebuild them, and how to use military lingo, at all of which Sonny excelled.

Frequently, Marie would ask Sonny for help and advice on radio operations and repair. In exchange, she corrected his Canadian accent to sound European-French.

In time, the team learned that they were to operate radios from Scotland to support the Allied invasion in Europe. The operation, code named "Fortitude South," decoyed the Germans into rationalizing that the main attack would materialize on the shortest route to France: Le Pas-de-Calais.

At this point, none of the operatives knew that the real invasion would land on the beaches of Normandy. They only knew General Patton would lead such an "invasion," but their commanders gave no timeframe. The team knew better than to ask.

With the exhausting days of training, Sonny fell asleep each night as soon as his head hit the pillow. A few times, someone speaking English in his ear awakened him during the night. He failed the repetitive exercise on four occasions by responding in English. Before long, however, he was replying in fluent French, even when roused out of a deep sleep.

During the arduous training, their duties became very clear: to speak in French and sometimes in English on the wireless, using scripts given to them by the intelligence specialists. The radio transmissions were mundane, with an occasional slip up about the upcoming attack on Pas-de-Calais, a mention of General Patton, or messages about stockpiling supplies. All were designed to lead the Germans to assemble a puzzle, so they had their troops in the wrong location at an assigned time.

It was April 16, 1944 when the major came into their briefing room and announced, "Listen up team. We have a problem."

Just *Who* Is Coming to Dinner?

Jack arrived at 7 p.m. to meet Emily and Gisele at The High Tide, the local restaurant and tavern they frequented. It was a locals' favorite that one didn't brag about for fear of not being able to secure a reservation. Jack entered the restaurant and surveyed the bar area. He found Emily and Gisele standing at the center of the bar. Emily waved to him; he walked up, planted a kiss on her cheek, and said to Gisele: "Nice to see you, glad you made it."

"We were talking before you got here," Emily said. "Gisele was telling me about her lecture, and I was telling her the story Dad told us back on New Year's Eve."

"Yeah, Dad told us quite a story about a secret mission behind enemy lines during World War II, Gisele," Jack said. "What do you think about all that?"

"It was common after the war that veterans would not speak of their service," Gisele said. "I would like to hear more about your father over dinner."

"I will tell you what I know," Jack said.

"He sounds like quite an ingenious man from what I gather from your beautiful wife," she said, acknowledging Emily.

"Aw, thank you, Gisele," Emily said. "You're beautiful too!"

Jack was about to make the obligatory comment about how lucky he was to be in the company of two beautiful women, when the host approached to lead them to their table.

Dinner was most enjoyable. Jack devoured prime rib prepared medium rare with garlic-mashed potatoes and steamed green beans. He washed it down with his favorite amber beer. Emily enjoyed a large chef salad chock-full of chicken, ham, cheese and eggs, which she paired with a chilled glass of

Chardonnay. Gisele ordered grilled halibut with asparagus and a glass of champagne.

"Gisele, why did you embark on such an arduous speaking tour?" Emily asked.

"I want to honor my grandfather, who gave his life in the war, and I hope to accomplish this by honoring those still alive who served behind enemy lines to free those oppressed by the Nazis," Gisele lowering her eyes.

"Forgive me for saying, but it seems a little bizarre to me that a young *German* woman is going around the country giving recognition to old soldiers who fought for the Allies," Jack felt compelled to point out.

"Not all Germans agreed with the war. My grandfather did not," Gisele said, looking at Jack with frosty blue eyes. "I have spent several years seeking those who served as my grandfather did. Many of these men and women are difficult to find. They still believe they must stay hidden and be secretive, but the war was long ago. My mission is to find those who are still alive to ensure that they receive their proper honor."

Gisele took a sip from her champagne flute and sighed.

"I agree with you, Gisele," said Emily, "they are all unsung heroes."

"Dad *is* my hero," Jack said. "Have you found many others like my father in your travels, Gisele?"

"Quite a few. I recognize them for their service in my special way. I'm glad to know your father is one such soldier I've sought," Gisele said. "Many veterans dislike public recognition."

Jack was about to ask Gisele about her special way of recognizing veterans when the server dropped their check. Gisele offered to share the tab, but Jack insisted on being her host.

"Can you stay for an after-dinner drink?" Jack asked Gisele. He felt he hadn't enough information from her about his father's covert service.

"No, I have to fly to Houston tomorrow for my next speaking engagement, and I still have to prepare. But perhaps when I get back? Please keep in touch. I would like to hear more about your father," Gisele said.

"I look forward to it," replied Jack.

He helped Gisele with her coat and walked her to a green Chevy Malibu. It appeared to be a rental vehicle.

After Gisele departed, Emily and Jack moved to the bar where bartender Bob regaled them with his nonstop jokes about subjects ranging from the Big Dig in Boston to job hunting and children. At about 11 p.m., closing time, the couple left the restaurant. The humid air hit them like a wall; sweat forming on their brows. As they approached their car, they noticed the front right tire was flat.

"Damn!" Jack cursed. "Just my luck these days."

"It's late. Bob is closing up. Maybe he can give us a ride home. I'll go ask him," Emily said.

Bob was more than happy to help. He gave them the phone number to the local gas station down the road to fix the tire.

They arrived home around 1 a.m., having survived a flat tire and a long wait for Bob to close up the restaurant. Tired and sated with good food and wine, they fell asleep.

The next morning Emily dropped Jack off at the gas station to wait for the tow truck driver armed with coffee and donuts for the mechanics. He informed them of his flat tire on the Durango. Jack jumped in the cab with the tow truck driver, who arrived about 20 minutes late. The cab and the driver smelled of stale fast food and cigarettes.

Ah well, Jack thought, *I only must survive about two miles of torture.*

As the mechanic lifted up the car and then started to remove the lug nuts, he looked at Jack.

"Hey buddy, this tire didn't go from a nail. Someone slashed it."

"Slashed on purpose? In this part of town? Could it have happened elsewhere?" Jack asked.

The mechanic shook his head. "No, this gash is too long," he said pointing to the tear.

"What are you saying?" Jack asked.

"Within thirty seconds after someone slit this tire, it was flat. No way you drove even two feet without noticing," the mechanic replied. "Get the police out here so you can get this covered by your auto insurance."

"Yeah, I guess you're right," Jack said. "Can you still change it and give me the tire?"

"Sure, no problem, mister," said the mechanic as he went back to removing the slashed tire.

Jack dialed the operator connected him to the town police desk. He explained what had happened to the dispatcher and informed an officer would be out there as soon as one was available.

"Can I get a timeframe?" Jack asked.

"Can't," the dispatcher said. "All the officers are in the field. One of them will be out as soon as they can," the dispatcher replied.

More waiting, Jack thought.

The mechanic finished his repairs. He handed Jack a bill.

"You can pay at the shop tomorrow." He said.

Jack debated about asking the mechanic about repairing the front passenger door while he waited but decided he should schedule an appointment.

About an hour later a police car pulled into the parking lot, the officer stepped out, pulling his pants up over his belly as he closed the door to his black and white patrol car.

Jack laughed to himself, "Here comes Sheriff Andy!"

"You Jack?" the patrolman queried. "That the car?"

"Yes, Officer," Jack replied. "Seems we had a tire slashed here last night; it's on the passenger side of the car and the mechanic has already replaced the tire.

The police officer examined the slashed tire. "Should have left the tire on the car, you might have destroyed some evidence. That is a nasty cut. No pocketknife did this. My hunch is it was a military, hunting or fishing knife."

"I wasn't thinking someone would do that," Jack said. "I wanted to replace the flat tire."

"You see anyone suspicious inside the restaurant?" the policeman asked.

"No," Jack replied, eager to end the conversation, "Just the usual suspects, err... just the usual crowd."

"There's not much I can do," the officer said. "I'll write up a report that you can pick up tomorrow at the station. You'll need that for your insurance company."

"Thanks for taking the time to come down here and write your report," Jack said.

"No problem. Have a good one," the officer said as he walked away and climbed into the squad car before driving away.

"Damn this frigging useless paperwork," the officer muttered as he tossed his notebook in the passenger seat.

"What a waste of two hours," Jack grumbled as he opened the hatch door of the SUV to store the slashed tire.

"Who on earth would slash my tire? Whoever they are, I hope they rot in hell for causing all this aggravation and expense. Once I report this to auto insurance, they'll raise our rates."

Channel Crossing

"We have just learned that we have lost a team that was attempting a very dangerous mission. We have just 48 hours to prepare a new team to complete their task," announced Major Smythe. "It is perilous and conceivable that you will not return alive, so I can only accept volunteers."

He briefed them on the details. Their mission was to deliver radios to the Free French and the Maquis partisans so they could respond to the fake radio transmissions sent by MI6 and Major Smythe's team.

"What happened to the last team?" Sonny asked.

"A German bomber sank their fishing boat as it left the harbor," Major Smythe replied, showing no emotion.

Marie was the first to raise her hand to volunteer. Sergio raised his hand thereafter. The two British agents whispered to each other.

Sonny hesitated.

"We need you," Marie whispered to Sonny.

Marie's right, Sonny agreed. *This may be my only chance to serve my country in this war.*

Within a few minutes, their entire team was onboard.

"Cameron and Horace, you will stay here in Scotland," Smythe said. "You will aid with transmissions and maintain contact with Marie, Sonny, and Sergio to coordinate radio drops and replacement part locations sent to them via coded messages.

The next two days passed. Two days of waiting for a rendezvous with a French fishing boat and its captain, Henri Gibert.

Major Smythe told the group that Henri was their team leader.

"Underneath his crusty exterior the man has a heart of gold," he said. "I learned this firsthand when I was one of several British soldiers he rescued at Dunkirk. At the time, he was a retired army sergeant who had taken up fishing. We've been friends since then. Remember what I told you—don't trust anyone?" Major Smyth said. "Well, Henri is an exception to that warning. You can trust him with your life, always."

"What will we do on arrival?" Marie asked.

"Henri will bring you to his farmhouse between Bergues and Dunkirk," Smythe said. "How are we to explain our presence?" Sergio asked.

"You and Sonny will assist Henri on the farm," Smythe replied. "You are relatives, displaced by the war."

"I can do that, "Sonny said. "I helped the local farmer in my town for several summers." "At night, your mission is to deliver radios to safe houses," Smythe said. "The rendezvous location will change daily to avoid attracting Jerry's attention."

The Scottish coast in spring was damp and chilly; the rain had stopped during the night and it was now only a drizzle. Sonny pulled his cap over his ears and buttoned his coat, sticking his hands in his pockets for warmth. As the salty sea air swirled around him. It chilled him to the bone through the layers of his clothing. Waves crashed on the beach. Swooped up by the wind, the water spattered his face. Sonny wiped his face and mouth with his handkerchief, tasting the strong sea salt. Mists swirled along the coastline like a surreal ghoul.

The team waited in silence for the boat to arrive. Sonny caught glimpses of the approaching fishing boat struggling through the sea swells. The North Atlantic was rough this time of a year. His stomach began to churn at the prospect of the trip across the channel. As the fishing boat came into view, Sonny observed that the vessel looked seaworthy for such a trip. The boat pulled up to an old worn dock. Sergio and Marie help tie ropes thrown by the fisherman to the poles that supported the frame.

Major Smythe greeted a grizzled man, somewhere around fifty years old, dressed in a fisherman's garb, a black beret, and rubber boots. He looked unperturbed by the damp air that gusted around him, nor the spray that hit his face, dripping off his white beard. His old beat-up coat was wet.

"*Mon amie, content de te voir!*" Smythe said. "I see Jerry hasn't got you yet."

"*Les Bosch* are slow and dimwitted," Henri said. The two men embraced, patting each other on the back.

"I know these two," Henri said, pointing at Sergio and Marie. "I do not recognize the boy."

"He has volunteered," Smythe said. "He is brilliant at radio construction and repair."

"I did not agree to bring someone so young to war," Henri said. "He will be a liability."

"*Je peux me débrouiller par moi-même,*" Sonny said.

"So, you speak my language," Henri said. "You say you can handle yourself, but can you handle the evil we are about to face?"

Sonny remained silent.

"I will take him, major," Henri said. "It is against my better judgment, but I will trust you know what you are doing."

"Thank you, Henri," Smythe said.

"If anyone asks, you are my son," Henri said to Sonny. "Do as I say at all times. If you don't, it could cost both of us our lives."

"*Oui, Papa,*" Sonny replied.

"*Très bien,*" Henri said. "We must go soon. There will be a full moon tonight and I don't want to be detected in the channel when it rises." Henri checked his pocket watch.

"Godspeed," Smythe said. "I want a daily report on your progress. Sergio, that will be your responsibility."

"Sir," Sergio said. Major Smythe and Henri slapped each other on the shoulder, saying their goodbyes. Not so long ago, Sonny floated on the Merrimack River in an old wooden boat with his friend Raymond, fishing for bullheads. Sonny had always enjoyed the water and loved to fish. He had vacationed every summer with his family at Cape Cod. The dark churning water of the Atlantic contributed to an unsettling perception of impending danger lurking in the gray vastness ahead.

Sonny climbed into the fishing boat, refusing the hand Henri offered him for support. His legs gave way as he slid on the slimy deck, falling headfirst into a pile of ropes entangled with fish heads.

Wiping himself off as he stood, smearing fish guts on his trousers, Sonny hid his red face as he walked over to a bench that circled the back of the fishing boat. Henri shouted out orders to release the ropes and as Sergio, Sonny, and Marie went into action. The thirty-foot fishing boat came off the dock. Its engines protested under the strain of pulling the heavy boat into deeper water. Diesel fumes from the pistons filled the air, mingling with the dense fog and the odor of rotten fish. *Boy, do I miss the smell of the pine trees when we fished from our old wooden boat on the Merrimack River*, Sonny thought as he sat, watching Henri spin the fishing boat around and rev up the engines to head out into the channel.

Full moon or not, the channel is no place to be in, day or night.

As if reading Sonny's thoughts, Henri said, "The *Kriegsmarine* have increased their patrols along the French coastline. We must be vigilant."

"Why the increased patrols?" Sonny asked.

"Rumors of an Allied invasion of the Calais coastline have surfaced," Henri said. "The rumors were generated from the success of the false information we have been feeding their intelligence."

"Our work has now made this trip more dangerous," Sergio said.

"It is a double-edged sword," Marie said. Henri's faithful service to the French Resistance began in 1940, when the British Army retreated in defeat across the English Channel from Dunkirk. A young intelligence officer named Scotty Smythe jumped into Henri's fishing boat, and as they crossed the channel, the two men talked through the night, shouting above the constant chugging of the diesel engines. Henri took Scotty and the five other British soldiers to England at great risk. So began the lifelong friendship between Brit Scotty Smythe and Frenchman Henri Gibert. Henri risked his life on many missions since that fateful crossing, transporting men and supplies across to isolated points on the Pas-de-Calais coastline. Henri knew he was not the only French fisherman involved with the Free France movement. It saddened him he had never had the privilege of meeting any of his counterparts. As they pulled out to sea, Marie said, "Sonny, come below with Sergio and me."

Henri overruled her, "Leave the boy with me at the helm. If we get stopped, he is my son."

Marie nodded in acknowledgement, disappearing below deck. "Remember Sonny, speak only French. If they stop the boat, they will speak English to you to trap you," Henri said.

"*Oui,*" Sonny promised. Sonny felt comfortable in Henri's company. He kept busy by helping Henri with mundane tasks on deck. They cleaned and wrapped fish in newspaper and dropped them into the hold. The fishing boat scudded along six-foot high swells. Henri recognized the flushed look on Sonny's face.

"Maybe you should get into a hammock, you will feel better," Henri said. Sonny rose. He gripped the brass ring on the trap door leading below and lifted the water-soaked hatch. He descended the ladder.

"Aren't you supposed to be with Henri?" Marie asked.

"Not feeling to good," He replied.

"Hammocks are over there," she said. "Rest up, you need to be well when we arrive."

"First time across the English Channel?" Sergio asked.

Sonny nodded in acknowledgement.

"You'll get used to it," Sergio said.

Sonny climbed in the hammock, queasy, hungry, and exhausted. He was soon asleep.

"Henri's got his work cut out for him with this young boy," Sergio said.

"*Oui, oui*, but he has courage," Marie said.

Sonny awoke after midnight to the echo of a German voice on a megaphone. Panicking, he tried to hustle out of the hammock, only to find he was further tangled in it. He saw Marie and Sergio sitting at the table, enveloped in swirls of cigarette smoke. Sonny saw through the dim light of the lantern they had been playing cards. Henri ducked his head through the trap door, calling to them to stay below, to stay calm and act normal.

The loud rumble of powerful engines approached, heralding a much larger boat.

And I deduced I was nervous before, Sonny thought, frozen in terror as his mind raced with the horrific possibilities of what might come next.

Heavy ropes thudded on the boat. Henri secured them to the fishing boat. Three Kriegmarines boarded Henri's boat's slick, fish-ridden deck.

Shucks, none of the Nazis slipped, thought Sonny.

A last set of boots land on the deck, followed by a click of heels.

Must be their officer, Sonny surmised.

Henri spoke to the Germans in his dry, chortling tone.

"What are you doing out at this hour?" the German officer asked in French.

"Catching what I can while my lazy friends at Dunkirk sleep," Henri replied with a laugh.

"Who's with you on this vessel?" the officer demanded.

"My son, a daughter and her husband," Henri said with no hesitation, as he moved toward and opened the trap door, calling his family up to meet the Germans. Sergio came on deck first, accompanied by Marie and Sonny. A German officer was standing next to Henri, two Kriegmarines with MG 40 machine guns stood behind them. Sonny's eyes widened.

I've seen those machine guns before, he reflected. *Those are the same weapons the FBI agents carried out of the French River Inn back in 1942.*

The German officer directed the two Kriegmarines to search the compartments below. He glanced at Marie and Sergio and then stared for a long moment at Sonny, as if to question this red-faced kid's relationship to the weather-beaten old man who claimed to be his father. Henri put his arm around Sonny and brought him to the Officer.

"Show your respect, my son." Henri said.

"*Ravie de vous rencontrer, monsieur,*" Sonny said.

Marie bit back a proud grin. The officer asked if their fishing trip had been fruitful. Henri nodded and Sonny opened the hatch to show the Germans their catch.

"Would you care to take some fish with you?" Marie asked.

"What's a woman doing on this fishing boat?" the officer asked.

Marie responded out of turn, "Father and I have been teaching Sonny the ins and outs of our business so he can take over the fishing boat one day."

"Marie's been my right arm on this boat since my other two sons died in the war," Henri said, glaring at Marie for her impertinence.

"It is time for her to get back to the kitchen," the *Kriegsmarine* officer said. Everyone laughed, except Marie who lowered her eyes under her beret.

The two Kriegsmarine*s* climbed onto the deck from below shaking their heads at the officer. The officer nodded back to them to get on back on the patrol boat, turning to Henri.

"I'll leave you to your fishing," he said, jumping onto the patrol boat. Sonny peered through the mist to get a good look at the German vessel. There were two manned 20 mm gun mounts fore and aft and there appeared to be at least five other crew members on board.

A few moments afterward, the team breathed a sigh of relief in unison as loud engines roared to life, powering away the enemy patrol boat, and leaving the smaller fishing boat rocking in its wake.

 The three team members returned below but didn't speak. Henri started the engines and steered towards the Calais coastline. An hour later, Henri came below to share their meager breakfast of pickled herring and stale bread.

"I am thrilled with how calm you were," he said to them, as he looked at Sonny.

Henri placed his arm on Sonny's shoulder.

"Sonny, when I met you yesterday, you were a boy. Today you came face to face with the enemy and you did not flinch. *Bien*! Promise me you will always remember to trust no one, except for your mother."

Then he paused. "Even then, you must ask for her credentials," he chuckled with a secretive wink.

Suspicions

A few months passed. Fall began to creep in with cool evenings encroaching earlier on warm days.

A great time of a year, in New England, Jack thought, sometimes wearing his coat, sometimes not.

With the slashed tire incident behind them, Jack and Emily settled into their routines once again. They continued to meet every Friday night at their favorite restaurant and bar. With no recurrence of tire slashing, they soon returned to feeling comfortable and safe.

After they finished dinner at home one evening, Jack turned on the news as they settled in separate leather recliners, each holding a glass of wine. The evening's news anchor led off with a special local news bulletin.

"This morning, the police found a man murdered in his east side apartment. Mr. Alvin Ulbert was a World War II veteran who served America in France and Germany with the Office of Strategic Services, the predecessor to today's Central Intelligence Agency," the news anchor announced.

"The police are investigating this crime and encourage anyone with any information to please call the crime hotline at 1-800-555-4779. All calls will be anonymous," the anchorman said.

Jack turned to Emily. "Who would murder a World War II veteran?"

Emily responded, "How sad."

The next evening, Jack and Emily turned on the national news while preparing dinner. The news anchor reported additional details about the murder of World War II veteran Alvin Ulbert. They followed his story with stories about the murders of three other World War II veterans in New York, Vermont, and Connecticut. After the news teams' reports, the anchor concluded the segment, calling the murders, "tragic, odd, and the ultimate insult to these American heroes and their families."

The murders riveted Jack. He felt the hair stand on its end on the back of his neck. After dinner, Jack raced to his computer in the basement to search for additional information about the murders of WWII veterans. *Something tells me these murders are not coincidental*, he muttered, gritting his teeth.

Jack began with a search for the obituaries of World War II veterans. That proved exhaustive. One story link reported that there were 1700 World War II veterans dying each day. So, he typed a search for *murdered* World War II veterans and sat holding his breath. A few links popped up. The first was an article in the *Globe*, a local newspaper.
Interesting, he thought as he clicked on the link.

It appeared to Jack that the television station used the newspaper article titled "Suspicious Deaths of Veterans" for their report. The article included a map of the United States with red dots highlighting where investigations were ongoing involving the suspicious deaths of World War II veterans.

A click on each red dot revealed the name of a victim and the date of death. All the victims had died within the past eleven months, Jack noted. He clicked yet another link, which displayed the veteran's full biography, including where he had served. One thing became crystal clear: *all* these veterans had served in France and Germany.

I should mention this to Dad, Jack thought, reaching for his cell phone, but then he hesitated. *Dad might get annoyed that I'm being nosy.* He recalled his father's chilly behavior on the ride home after Gisele's speaking engagement about World War II veterans who had served in France and Germany.

Jack sat upright, thinking back to his father's tearful confession on New Year's Day: "I could tell no one, because if

I'm still here, so are they—and I didn't want to expose my family to danger or retaliation."

I won't say anything to Dad, Jack thought, *but I've got to check this out. My gut instinct tells me there's something screwy in St. Louis about these suspicious deaths.*

The next morning after Emily left for work, Jack called the *Globe* reporter who wrote the article, asking for a meeting to discuss his thoughts over coffee.

Gisele should know about this too, Jack thought. *She's an expert on this subject; perhaps I should invite her too, so they can put their heads together.*

"I think I'll call the newspaper first, meet the reporter, and then go from there," he said, talking out loud.

The phone call to Ben Townley, the *Globe* reporter, was fruitful.

"I have some interesting facts that my dad told me New Year's Day this year about serving behind enemy lines in Germany and France during World War II. My dad and I attended a talk by a German woman named Gisele Toffler at the local Elks Club last month. Gisele said her grandfather worked for the German postal service during World War II and was a double agent for the Allied Forces."

Jack told Ben how Gisele had said she was touring the United States to share her grandfather's story, while providing long overdue recognition to the Americans who served in the war.

Townley told Jack he was eager to hear more. He said he could meet Jack at about 10 a.m. the following morning at The Green Leaf coffee shop across the street from the newspaper's offices.

"Sounds great," Jack replied, as he clicked the *end* button on his cell phone. Jack didn't know where the meeting would lead, but his mind swirled with thoughts of World War II spies.

Jack had always fancied himself a fine writer. He often envied writers who came out with the "big story."

What the heck, I don't have a job right now. Maybe I could use this time to write a book about World War II spies, he thought, stroking Sassy, who lay next to his chair on the cool cement in his basement office. Sassy cocked her head and wagged her tail, as if she liked her dad being a novelist.

Jack spent the afternoon landscaping, as usual. Cooling off with a glass of iced tea, he searched his office for Gisele's business card, to no avail. I must have left it somewhere else, he thought, heading upstairs to check the den and kitchen. He thought of the Elks Club website. Jack returned to his computer and pulled up the notice about Gisele's talk. Bingo! Gisele's contact information was on the web page!

Jack dialed Gisele's number. But unlike the first time when he had called Gisele and she'd picked up, this time her phone just rang and rang. What seemed strange to Jack was that the ring tone sounded old fashioned, like something from the 1960s. *Maybe she is forwarding her calls to a landline somewhere in a rural area since she's speaking all over the country,* he thought.

Jack left Gisele a voicemail explaining his meeting the next morning with *Globe* reporter Ben Townley and invited her to join them or at least conference call with them.

When Emily got back from work that evening, Jack did not mention any of his calls. He figured she would only discourage his "new adventure," and cajole him again to focus more on finding a new job.

Until that great job comes along, this new adventure is just what I need to keep my brain from turning into mush, Jack thought.

The next morning, he awoke early to make breakfast for Emily.

"What's the occasion? Is it my birthday?" she asked.

"Funny!" he shot back, "Why must my wife think I have an ulterior motive when I want to make her a special breakfast?" Jack asked.

"This was sweet of you, Jack, but I have to leave right now for an early meeting, so I can't sit down and eat this feast, but I'll take that toast to go," she said, kissing him on the cheek.

As he heard Emily drive away, Jack sat down and devoured the eggs and bacon he had prepared for her. He drank the orange juice and glanced at the yellow rose in the vase. *That was a nice touch*, Jack thought. *She was in such a hurry; I don't think she noticed, though. Maybe she'll notice the rose at dinner tonight.*

Jack noted that he had not yet heard from Gisele.

She's busy on her speaking tour, he thought. *Gisele's a strange one anyway, a German woman going around the country talking about her grandfather's double agent service in World War II and giving recognition to American veterans.*

A horrible thought crossed Jack's mind; he put his glass of orange juice down with a thud, feeling nauseous. *Nah*, he dismissed the thought, *Gisele's paying tribute to WWII veterans, not murdering them.*

Looking at the clock, Jack realized it was already 8 a.m. He had better get moving. After a quick shower, he decided not to shave his two-day-old beard, thinking an unkempt look was more appropriate for a budding novelist. Jack jumped into his 1998 Dodge Durango, looking over at the rope holding the passenger door closed. *I've got to get that damn door fixed*, Jack thought. *Maybe I can take it to the same gas station that replaced the slashed tire. That mechanic seemed to know his stuff.*

It was a quick seven-mile drive downtown to the coffee shop since rush hour traffic had already subsided. All Jack had to deal with were the old geezers who were driving like they were cruising after Sunday church service like in the old days. No sooner than he cursed at the offending seniors as he changed lanes to pass them, Jack would chide himself, thinking *that'll be me one day.*

Jack pulled up to the coffee shop. He found a parking space in front but took a few minutes to parallel park. After a few tries he left the SUV sticking its rear out into the street. "Close enough," he grunted in defeat.

Jack opened the door to the coffee shop and glanced around, but no other customers were in the shop, except for a ruddy-faced middle-aged gentleman behind the counter.

"Morning" the barista announced, "Can I get you anything?"

"Hi" Jack replied, "I'm waiting for someone, but a medium cup of regular coffee would be fine, with cream and sugar," he added. Jack was not a fan of the froufrou coffees as he called them, preferring a regular cup of joe.

"That'll be $1.50. The cream, sugar, and stirrers are on the counter," the barista said.

Jack paid his tab, dropping a few quarters in the tip jar.

Even if I'm unemployed, tipping for good service is good karma, he thought.

Jack sat down and began leafing through a newspaper a previous customer had left on the table. Just then, Ben, the reporter, walked up behind him. Startled, Jack spilled coffee down the front of his shirt.

Oh great, Jack thought, *I've made a fine first impression.*

"Jack, I presume," Ben noted with a kid-like grin. Ben was in his mid-thirties, just shy of six feet, with sandy brown hair and glasses.

He looks like Bill Gates, thought Jack.

"I just got some coffee; do you want any?" Jack asked.

"No thanks, just finished my second cup, that's enough for me; I'm hyper enough without caffeine," Ben said.

The two men chatted for a while about golf, computers, and baseball before Ben took out a small notebook and pen from his jacket and approached the purpose of their meeting.

"So, you saw my map on our web page?" Ben asked Jack.

"Yes, I've doing some research on my dad. I didn't know he had served behind enemy lines in World War II. When I read your article and saw your map, my hair stood up on end," Jack admitted.

"My editor asked me last week to take the map down because of outrage from some victim's families. If I had taken it down last week, we might never have had the chance to connect," said Ben.

"The article came about because of the research I was doing on aging World War II veterans. I had no idea we were losing at least 1700 a day, so I wrote an article about that. Then I started seeing random reports from the Associated Press and Reuters about suspicious deaths of World War II veterans across the country—that's when I started digging deeper, and noticed a disturbing trend," Ben said, looking down at his notebook.

"Which was?" Jack asked.

"I discovered that a significant demographic of World War II veterans was *not* dying of natural causes. What's *even more* curious is that *all* those who had died amid suspicions of foul play had served in France and Germany were all connected with partisan movements or special operations during the war," Ben said.

Jack felt sick to his stomach.

Ben's turn to Jack for answers. "So, what information do you have for me that might be useful in a follow-up article?" Ben asked Jack.

Realizing he was making a big mistake talking to the reporter, Jack lied.

"I'm doing some research for my doctorate about special operations during World War II, and I needed an interesting lean. Your map seemed perfect," Jack said.

"Well, I guess you could use it, but I'm taking it off the website today since my editor insists that I must, or risk losing my job. I would be careful about using it. That map seems to have caused nothing but trouble for everybody since we first published it," Ben cautioned.

Ben leafed through his notebook and frowned. "You said you had some feedback to share with me about your dad's time in France and Germany during World War II," he said.

"I know little about my dad's time there, to be honest," Jack said. "But I've been curious about it, which is why I made it part of my MBA research. I have so many unanswered questions."

"What research have you done?" Ben asked.

"Your article was very helpful, and I learned a lot from Gisele's talk."

"Ah, Gisele," Ben said, writing in his notebook. "I've been researching her background and her grandfather's purported service history but have hit a brick wall in finding anything that corroborates her story, even now in unclassified records," Ben said.

"I've been trying to arrange an interview with Gisele for weeks. But she's always off speaking somewhere and hasn't returned my phone calls or emails," Ben complained.

"My wife Emily and I had dinner with Gisele the other night," Jack volunteered. "In fact, I left her a voicemail to join us this morning, but she didn't get back to me. I thought the two of you should compare notes because she's interviewed so many veterans."

Ben expressed his disappointment that he couldn't learn more from Jack about his father's World War II experiences. "Perhaps you could ask your dad if he'd be willing to talk with me," he asked Jack, putting away his notebook and pen.

Ben stood up, saying he needed to get back to his office to finish an article for the next day's newspaper before he got into any more trouble with his editor. The men shook hands and Ben left.

Jack sat down again. His coffee was cold, but not as chilled as the sinking feeling in his stomach. *I did the wrong thing by chickening out on telling Ben what Dad told me. I should have shared dad's story with Ben, so he could add it to his report,* Jack lamented.

At about 6:30 p.m. that evening, Ben Townley entered the newspaper's parking garage and stepped into the elevator. Exiting on the third level, he pulled out his cell phone, dialed a few numbers and waited.

"I've got updated information on Code Name Sonny and the Butcher's offspring. Let me know when we can meet." Stuffing the phone into his jacket pocket, Ben fished in his pant pockets for his car keys, unaware of the figure hiding behind the steel beam near his car.

That night's eleven o'clock television news hour led off with a special local news bulletin, showing police cordoning off a crime scene in a parking garage.

The broadcast reporter announced that "Police found thirty-four-year-old *Globe* reporter Ben Townley shot near his car in the newspaper's parking garage at about 7 p.m. tonight. The victim did not survive. Police suspect a robbery attempt that went awry because Townley's briefcase, wallet, watch, and cell phone were missing. *Globe* publishers have offered a $50,000 reward to anyone offers information leading to the arrest and conviction of the murderer.

Jack sat in an almost catatonic state for hours after the eleven o'clock news concluded. At about 2 a.m., Emily awoke with a start, surprised to find Jack's side of the bed empty. She turned on lights in the bedroom and hallway and went downstairs, surprised to see Jack sitting in the den with the television turned on to a late-night show. Some guy with a British accent was interviewing a celebrity.

That's odd, Emily thought. *Jack is not a fan of this show.*

Turning the television off, Emily turned and walked towards Jack. That's when she noticed the broken wine glass on the floor next to Jack's favorite leather recliner. Her eyes widened in horror when she observed her husband sitting in shock with his eyes wide open, oblivious to her and their surroundings.

My God, I think Jack's had a stroke, she thought, rushing to his side.

"There's been another murder," she heard Jack mumble.

Hidden places

Even the rocking of the hammock in the dark berth hadn't lulled Sonny to sleep. His veins were still twitching from their encounter with the German patrol boat. He walked over to the galley, hoping to find a hot cup of coffee and something to eat. All he could find in the galley was a jar of herring and a jug of wine. He almost reached for the wine to calm his nerves. Sonny longed for a hot sip of his Mom's great coffee with cream and sugar. His stomach groaned with hunger as he salivated at the memory of the huge helpings of bacon, eggs, and toast he devoured daily at home.

Sonny came up on deck at 4 a.m. as the boat's engines slowed. They were entering a harbor filled with boats of all sizes. In the distance, he saw houses in varying shapes and sizes, all with red tile roofs.

Soon those families will sit down to a great hot breakfast, Sonny mused, missing his family even more. Henri came from behind him, surveying the familiar harbor.

"Time to wake the others," Henri directed Sonny.

Sonny went below to retrieve them.

Marie and Sergio joined them on deck as they moored at the beach on the secluded southeast side of the harbor, away from the main docks, which were controlled by the enemy. Henri left them to fetch the horses and wagon while the three of them collected the fish they had packed in newspapers and loaded them onto the skiff.

They formed a relay chain to load the fish into the wagon. Marie and Sergio climbed into the back.

"Sonny, ride with me up front," Henri instructed.

They headed down a bumpy dirt road towards Henri's farmhouse. Now and then, Henri and Sonny locked eyes as they noticed deep ruts in the road that had been created by tank tracks.

"It looks like the *Boche* have been busy while we were at sea," Henri said.

Uneven roads made the wagon ride seem to last for hours, but in fact it was less than forty-five minutes before they completed the three kilometer journey to Henri's farmhouse, which was at the southwest of the small fishing village. The house and compound stood at the end of a long cobblestone lane flanked by olive trees, with bougainvillea and trumpet vines climbing the sidewalls. A courtyard had a small fountain with pots filled with cascading flowering plants lining the front porch.

As they pulled up, Henri announced that the property had been in his wife's family for five generations.

"If the farm was in the village, it would belong to the *Bosch* by now," Henri said.

"They don't take homes in the country?" Sonny asked.

"Too much in the open," Henri said. "They fear snipers. The town provides protection from that.

"Makes sense," Sonny said.

"My wife Bridget never complained about long wagon rides," Henri said. "She loved it out here."

"Is she here at the farm?" Sonny asked.

Henri was silent for a moment.

"She died in the war, when the *Boche* bombed our hospital where she was nursing the wounded.

"I am sorry," Sonny said. "Are you here alone?"

"My sister Antoinette came to live with me two years ago after her husband Maurice died in an act of terror."

"That must be nice," Sonny said.

"Not really, Antoinette runs our household and farm with an iron fist," he chuckled.

The door to the farmhouse swung open and two cocker spaniels dashed out, circling. Behind them, a woman wearing a long black skirt and white blouse, and her blond hair poking through her bonnet, walked to them. She rubbed her hands on her white apron as she approached.

Antoinette kissed Henri on both cheeks and ushered her guests to enter the house and wash up.

"Breakfast is getting cold," she admonished, smiling when she saw the gleam in Sonny's eyes at the mention of food. She directed one of the farm hands to retrieve the fish from the wagon, ordered the stable boy to water and feed the horses, and led the group into the house.

Antoinette held out warm wet towels to each of the new arrivals and directed them through kitchen doors. The aroma of savory, intoxicating smells of food filled the room.

They sat at an old handmade blackened table with tall wooden chairs.

No one spoke, as everyone was ravenous. A thick soup filled with seafood and vegetables followed a smoked trout starter with crusty bread topped with Normandy butter. The main course was a cross between a quiche and a frittata, filled with ham, eggs, mushrooms, broccoli, and cheese. The meal was delicious, and the coffee was strong and sweet.

Sonny devoured his food and asked for seconds, oblivious to the chuckles of his team members and Antoinette's delighted grin.

His stomach full and his equilibrium returning to normal, Sonny felt very drowsy.

Sensing Sonny's sated mood and exhaustion, Henri urged Antoinette to show the three charges to their rooms so they could freshen up and rest.

On his bed, Sonny found a clean black beret, a pair of khaki trousers, undergarments, socks and two white shirts. On a peg on the wall was a tweed woolen jacket that looked well worn. In the corner he found a pair of farm work boots, which also looked like they had seen a lot of use.

Sonny cleaned up at the sink stand from a jug of fresh warm water, towels, and soap that Antoinette had provided. He folded his old clothes and set them in a corner near the bedroom door. Sonny dressed in his new clothes and tumbled into bed. He was soon sound asleep.

At about five that afternoon, Sonny awoke to a quiet knock on his door.

"*Entrée, s'il vous plaît,*" he responded. Antoinette stood at the door with a tray laden with finger sandwiches, cheese and bread, pastries and a pot of hot tea with cream and sugar.

"We did not wake you for lunch because you were sleeping," she said.

"Breakfast was scrumptious, Madame, and I promise not to miss another one while I'm here," Sonny said.

His hostess smiled with pleasure at the sincere compliment.

Sonny was famished. He dived into his feast under the appreciative, watchful eyes of his hostess.

"When you are ready, Henri and your friends are waiting for you in the study," Antoinette said as she closed the door behind her.

Less than fifteen minutes later, Sonny joined the others in the study. Sergio was all in black, a gray wool cap shielding his face as he sat at the library table poring over maps. Beside him, Marie was in black pants and a cream tunic, her black hair pulled back under her black beret. A tan coat was slung over her chair. Henri sat in the captain's chair, smoking a pipe and reading a book.

Henri looked up when Sonny stood in the ornate double doors of the library.

"Put on your coat, young man, I want to give you a little tour of the grounds," Henri said. Sergio and Marie acknowledged his presence but didn't volunteer to join them. Henri led Sonny through the back door of the farmhouse, pointing to the vegetable and herb gardens and the beehives as they walked past them. They walked through the stables and past the chicken coops and on to a pasture where a few goats were grazing. A few minutes later, they came to a forested area with a narrow, visible dirt trail leading into the woods.

Henri turned onto the trail and Sonny followed. So did the five ever watchful dogs that had dashed out through a hole in their pen when they noticed their master going for a walk.

After walking for about ten minutes in silence, the trail ended at a group of tall, unkempt bushes. Henri spoke to the dogs, and they ran along the dirt trail towards their pen.

Henri used a stick to part the bushes, revealing a grotto.

"This used to be an old wine cellar," Henri explained as he opened the big old wooden doors. A strong smell of sulfur permeated the air as Henri struck a match to light a lantern. They were in a cave, in an area about twelve feet long and eight feet wide, with a beam ceiling seven feet high. Henri paused, holding out the lantern in front of him to break through the impenetrable darkness.

"The front area of this cave will be your regular meeting place every night," Henri said. "There is a field close by and my men will pick up the radio parts flown in by the supply courier and bring them here. We will place them in that wall cupboard on the left," he pointed with the lantern to a large knotty pine cabinet.

"You will arrive here by 7 p.m. to assemble the radios. Your contact will be here at 9 p.m. to escort you to your rendezvous with various partisan groups. I want you back at the farmhouse no later than midnight, since *le Bosch* have imposed a curfew in the entire region," Henri said.

He moved forward in the cave, motioning for Sonny to join him. Sonny recognized wine bottles stacked in racks and others lying flat in long rows on the dirt floor. Henri pushed at a rack of wine bottles and the rack sprung forward a crack.

Pushing the wine rack doorway further, Henri motioned Sonny forward into the hidden space and closed the secret doorway behind them. He guided Sonny through a winding tunnel, holding up the lantern to light their way.

Sonny noticed small crevices filled with food supplies in the walls of the cave. In other areas, they had carved storage spaces to a height of about three feet to house weapons, ammunition, beds and linen supplies; provided by local farmers for resistance groups needing a place to hole up.

Sonny spied different types of weapon in the underground stash, from the French Army standard rifles such as the World War I rifle as the *Fusil Berthier* Mle 1916, to British Sten submachine guns and Lee-Enfield No. 1 Mk. III rifles. He had spent hours after school pouring over arms manuals at the state guard unit, studying European weapons.

Henri explained that they had hidden some weapons in the cave after the French Army surrendered; some were from private collections, but most came from supply drops and special operations groups passing through the area.

"You can't be too picky when you can't go to the local market to buy what you need to fight your enemy," Henri said with a chuckle in the darkness.

"We've been walking through this maze for a few minutes, but something tells me that when we get to the end of this cave, we'll be standing under the farmhouse study," said Sonny.

Henri just grunted his pleasure at Sonny's acute sense of direction.

Henri paused at a dead end in the tunnel, training the lantern at the ceiling, searching for a specific spot. He pulled at a board above his head. A trap door opened, and a rope ladder fell towards them.

Turning to Sonny, Henri said, "We will climb this ladder and find ourselves on a hearth behind the fireplace in the study." He then extinguished the lantern's flame, leaving them in total darkness. Sonny preceded Henri up the ladder. With a small thud, the trap door closed. Sonny heard the clicking of the fake fireplace opening. They entered the study to a rush of fresh air and knowing looks from Marie and Sergio.

"Guess Sonny figured it out too, eh?" Marie said.

A few minutes later, Antoinette announced supper, which was just as delicious as the breakfast and afternoon repast on which Sonny had feasted. After they had dined, the group retired to the library, where Henri served each of them a glass of Cognac.

"Let's propose a toast to *Liberté*," said the disheveled French fisherman, as they raised their glasses.

"*¡Salud!*" said Sergio.

An Old Friend

Jack trembled. Had he caused the death of *Globe* reporter Ben Townley? It didn't seem logical, but they had met for coffee the very day someone murdered the reporter. Ben had talked about his map bringing negative attention, and about pressure from his editor to remove it from the website.

The men who died on the map Ben had created were all special operations veterans. Maybe Ben had made an enemy by creating that map. Maybe the Nazis who were still alive were on a hunt for the men who had bested them. It all seemed like some crazy spy movie.

His thoughts turned to his dad. Could *he* be in danger? *I'd better talk to Dad. This is way beyond anything I've ever dealt with. If Dad was in special operations, he'll know what to do.*

Jack got in his Durango and drove to his parents' house, which sprawled on nine acres of land surrounded by woods on three sides. He had always loved their country estate growing up. Memories of warm family gatherings at birthdays and vacations went through his mind, like a photo library coming to life.

It was just twenty minutes to his parent's home, but today the drive seemed much longer. Jack worried about the remote location of his parent's home. His imagination ran wild.

What if something happened to my parents? Jack thought. *I'd never be able to forgive myself. Dad insisted that I keep this to myself, but I ignored his warnings. I wish Dad had never told me.*

Tears welled up in his eyes.

Jack's fears revved into full gear when he saw a blue Ford Taurus parked in his parents' driveway. It looked like a rental vehicle; he confirmed this on the dash, which displayed the local airport's sticker. A moment of terror-struck Jack.

Am I too late? he thought.

To his immense relief, his father stepped outside to greet him before he could even step onto the porch. "So, what's the big honor?" Joe asked.

"Nothing Dad, I was in the area. Figured I'd stop by and say hi," Jack said trying to sound nonchalant.

"Come on in, there's someone I want you to meet," Joe said.

Jack walked back to the passenger side door of his Durango, jarring it open, just enough to reach through the gap created by the rope still tied inside for the coffee he had been sipping. "Gotta get this damn door fixed," he grumbled for perhaps the eightieth time as he shoved the passenger door closed.

"Door still broken?" Joe asked, "The money offer to fix it still stands."

"Nah," Jack chortled, "Just need to get off my lazy butt to get it done is all."

As they walked in the house, Jack smelled the welcoming aroma of coffee brewing.

"Need a refresher?" Joe asked as he pointed to Jack's cup.

"Sure," Jack replied.

Jack queried, "Dad, whose car..." His voice trailed as he received his answer before he had finished asking the question. A man who looked to be about ten years older than his dad emerged from the den, walking towards them with a cane in his left hand.

"Hello, Jack, your dad has told me so much about you. It's a pleasure to meet you. My name is William Fowlie Smythe, but my friends call me Scotty," he said with a British accent as he shook Jack's hand.

"Scotty and I worked together during the war," Joe added. "Sure had some interesting experiences, didn't we?" Joe said.

"We did, mate. We did," Scotty said.

"Is this same thing you told me about at New Year's, Dad?" Jack asked.

"Yep, it is." Joe replied.

"Scotty and I met in Scotland for a mission called Operation Skye. His job was to train new groups for relaying fake transmissions to confuse the Germans about the Allied High Command strategy. They then deployed many members of these groups to France to deliver radios and keep them in good operating condition," Joe explained.

"The Nazis had a nasty trick to ferret out Allied spies among French civilians. They would wake you up when you were sleeping and whisper in English in your ear. If you responded in English, you were dead meat. Scotty busted me as I responded in English, groggy when being roused from a deep sleep," Joe said.

"How did you get past that?" Jack asked.

"Without the help from a fellow agent named Marie, I'd never have made it," Joe said, sighing, as if recalling a sad memory.

"My new trainees came to me with their nappies on, your dad included," Scotty said winking at Jack.

"Nappies?" Jack cast a quizzical look at his dad.

"Diapers," Joe muttered, his face turning red in embarrassment.

"Lucky for your dad, another trainee, a young French woman on our team had a soft spot for a certain red-faced French Canadian American young man. Marie practiced French with Sonny here until he was speaking it even when awoken from a sound sleep."

"Marie was an incredible woman, sharp as a whip, with a terrific sense of humor. And she was a real beauty, with blue-black hair and green eyes. I miss her," Joe said.

Marie must have meant a great deal to these two men, Jack realized as he saw the two men exchange long, sad looks.

Another thought struck Jack. *Scotty must be a very close friend of Dad's. I heard no one outside our family call Dad by his childhood nickname; Sonny.*

Jack sat looking at the two men.

Scotty broke the solemn silence with wry British humor to lighten the mood.

"The Americans on our team thought they had it bad with the Nazi mind games. But even with something as mundane as eating, the Nazis picked us Brits out," he said.

"Why is that?" Jack asked.

"Using a knife to eat the British way was a dead giveaway, every pun intended," Scotty replied.

"So, what brings you all the way from the United Kingdom?" Jack asked Scotty, changing the subject.

"Such a pleasant surprise!" Joe offered.

"My wife Gertrude and I came to visit her relatives in the area, and I seized the opportunity to catch up on old times with your dad," Scotty explained.

Joe ushered them back to the den. Jack noted that Scotty leaned on his cane. "I don't need this," Scotty guffawed pointing to his cane, "but it helps get me out of going to market with the Mrs."

Jack noticed that Scotty was frowning, as if pondering whether to bring up a private matter the two men had to discuss in Jack's presence.

"Sonny, it appears our old foe is causing problems again, but this time it's his granddaughter on some crazed mission to exact brutal revenge against those who she thinks killed her grandfather. She's been making the rounds throughout America, seeking out…"

Scotty began to say when Joe interrupted: "Maybe we should talk in private."

Scotty looked his friend in the eye.

"Your son has already met the lady, Sonny. It's too late to keep secrets from him. Jack and his wife are in danger, too, and they should hear this."

"Damn it, Scotty, is Gisele *The Butcher's* granddaughter?" Joe asked.

"Yes, she is targeting World War II veterans who served in France behind enemy lines. Gisele has been eliminating other teams. She has been interviewing veteran after veteran, hoping for a lead to us. She knows about you, Sonny, but she doesn't know your last name, or where you live. I suspect she'll use Jack here to find and kill you."

Jack felt as if he was about to faint. He blurted out, "Crap! Emily and I met Gisele for dinner the other night."

"Jack, have you seen Gisele since her talk at the Elks Club? Did you tell her where we live?" Joe asked.

"No, Dad, but she has our phone number and Emily gave her a business card. Emily uses her maiden name at work."

Jack explained his investigation, their dinner with Gisele, and recent events including his meeting with a reporter named Ben Townley. He began to panic.

When Jack mentioned Ben's map of the United States showing the locations of the murders and suspicious deaths of World War II veterans, Scotty interrupted.

"Where is it? I want to see it," he asked.

"In the car. I'll go get it," Jack said. "I'm so sorry, Dad," he said as he got up, hugging his father's shoulders.

"Not your fault kid—go get that map," Joe said.

Jack rushed out to the car and grabbed the map from the back-seat floor where he had tossed it the day of his meeting with Ben Townley. The map was wrinkled and had a small coffee stain, but everything was still legible. Jack handed the map to his father who looked at it with intense interest.

"Scotty, I'll bet most of these guys were behind the lines. I recognize a few names," Joe said.

Scotty reached out his hand for the map.

"Give it here, lad." Joe handed the map to Scotty, who took reading glasses from his shirt pocket. "Jack, please tell me again, *who* gave you this map?"

"A reporter for the *Globe* newspaper by the name of Ben Townley, around his mid-thirties. He kind of looked like a younger Bill Gates," Jack explained. "Ben said that when he was doing research, it startled him to learn how many World War II veterans were dying of unnatural causes. So, he created this map to accompany his investigative report about suspicious deaths and murders of those veterans."

"Ben also said his editor was getting a lot of heat from readers who objected to the maps and the story. He said his editor had asked him to remove the map from the website. Ben also asked if Dad would talk with him for a follow-up story. His full report is online if you'd like to read it. That's all the information I have—except the same evening of our meeting, someone shot him in the newspaper's parking garage. The TV report said police thought it was a robbery."

"Townley's killing was no coincidence, Sonny," Scotty revealed. "Townley was CIA. A few moments before someone murdered him, he called his team leader to alert the agency that your father's identity was discovered. That's why they brought me back for this visit: to warn you. Retired and all, the agency knows our enemies who may watch us will view this meeting as old friends reminiscing. But with Gisele circling like a vulture, they are wrong. We have to get a plan together."

"Shouldn't the CIA be dealing with Gisele rather than you two?" Jack asked.

"Now that Gisele has taken out Townley, one of their own, I'm sure the agency will step up their efforts to apprehend Gisele. But your father and I are who she is after, so we should be prepared," Scotty replied.

Joe went to a cabinet to reach for three snifters.

"No sense in letting the good stuff sit," he muttered, as he plunked the glasses down on the counter. "Everything's going to hell in a hand basket; we might as well enjoy this while we can."

The *good stuff* was one hundred and twenty-year-old whiskey Joe saved for special occasions. That bottle had been off limits as far back as Jack could remember. Jack watched in stunned disbelief as his father pulled what Emily called *The Bottle*, from the shelf.

"Dad, where's Mom?" Jack asked, afraid for his mother's well-being.

"She's out shopping. She's okay for now," Joe said.

"You should get her out of the area until we finish this, Sonny," Scotty warned. "Gertrude is with her relatives here; I'm sure she'd love to see Claire again. Let's arrange that so they are both safe."

"Can't imagine someone brave enough to mess with those two broads," Joe said.

In the past, Scotty and Trudy had vacationed with Joe and Claire, for pleasure, intermingled with business.

"Jack might as well hear this, my friend," Scotty said to Joe. "It's best he knows we might need his help."

"I don't want my son used as a decoy," Joe said.

"We have no choice. Jack is the only one in contact with her, and this is our only lead," Scotty countered. "I am sorry; *he* has to be the one."

Jack interjected, "It's okay, Dad. We've met her already and I can handle it. Besides, I feel responsible for putting you in harm's way."

"Trust me, Jack, these *people* are not ones you tinker with," Joe said, his mind clogged with sad snapshots of the friends he had lost to The Butcher's slaughter.

"We need a plan," Scotty repeated, moving to the library table. "If she's like her father, we have but a small window of opportunity before she vanishes and takes on her next disguise."

For the next few hours the men discussed all the options open to them and the best way to trap Gisele before she could kill again.

Joe and Scotty agreed that Jack and Emily would meet Gisele again for dinner, but they would follow her from the restaurant. Scotty would tail her since she knew what Joe looked like.

"Sure you can remember to drive on the right side of the road?" Joe teased Scotty.

"The left side is the right side," Scotty retorted. "You Americans just don't get it right."

Jack almost smiled at their bravado. These two old men—murder targets—were taking care of business. Jack realized that for men like Scotty and Joe, who had lived their entire lives with this kind of danger hanging over their heads, retirement was *not* an option. World War II may have ended over fifty years ago, but it prepared them to clean up unfinished business in the new millennium.

"Just act normal, Jack," Joe said.

"I don't know what's normal anymore," Jack said.

"Once you set a place and time with Gisele, let us know," Scotty said.

"Preferably in a popular restaurant on a busy street, so Scotty could blend into the crowd," Joe said.

"I know just the place," Jack said.

Joe handed Jack a cell phone.

"Call our house using this phone, just in case she has your landline at home tapped," he instructed.

"How could she tap our phone?" Jack asked.

"She's well versed in the spy game, Jack," Scotty said. "Do not make the mistake of underestimating her."

As Jack walked to his Durango to head back home, he did not notice the black sedan with shaded windows that drove away.

The blonde woman inside smiled. *I've got you, Sonny!*

Killing of Innocents

After drinking their Cognac, Henri told Marie and Sergio to get ready; their contacts would arrive at the farmhouse within minutes. He motioned for Sonny to stay in the study while he escorted Marie and Sergio to the foyer. While they donned their coats, he gave them their weapons, last-minute instructions, and advice. Antoinette came to wish them well, handing each a baguette filled with ham and cheese and wrapped in a large cloth napkin.

After they departed, Henri and Sonny returned to the grotto to assemble two radios for Free French units in the local countryside. They worked by the dim light of a lantern in the cold, musty cave—a difficult task, but secrecy from the Nazis was imperative. The Gestapo had their spies everywhere. Topmost in Sonny's mind was Henri's warning: *Remember, Sonny; trust no one.*

Antoinette tapped on the fireplace three times, signaling to Henri and Sonny down below in the cave to stop working; it was near curfew time.

The following day passed much like the first. After breakfast, Sonny kissed Antoinette on both cheeks, thanking her for spoiling him with wonderful home-cooked meals. *God was watching over me when he placed me in Henri and Antoinette's care*, Sonny thought. *It's like I have a mother and father here, 2000 miles from home.*

That evening's supper was comprised of potato soup with crusty bread, a bowl of bouillabaisse, a small glass of red wine, and cheese for dessert. Sonny inhaled the meal as usual. Henri chuckled as he watched the young man devour his food.

"Easy Sonny, you may regret having a full stomach tonight."

As the fireplace mantle clock stuck 7 p.m., Henri and Sonny re-entered the faux fireplace, dropped the ladder, and walked into the dark, damp cave to retrieve the radios and set out for the night's mission. Each grabbed a radio, a rifle, a belt of ammunition, and some rations for the night's journey to the Free French camps. They made their way to a part of the cave Sonny hadn't noticed before. Henri pushed at a rock and climbed out of the cave. He stood for a long moment as he scanned the countryside. When he was sure that they were clear, he reached out his hand to pull Sonny out of the cave.

Sonny looked around; he did not see the farmhouse. He buttoned his coat and followed Henri down a winding path. Henri assessed Sonny, assuring himself that they could pass for father and son traveling on foot through the countryside.

At the very least, many Nazis will die before they can kill us, Henri thought, a ferocious look crossing his face.

Sonny questioned his quizzical look; Henri just waved his hand, shrugging as if to say, "Nothing."

No need to frighten this fine young man, Henri thought.

"Follow me," he said.

After about fifteen minutes, Henri paused in a small clearing that looked man-made and out of place. He stopped, sat down, and took a drink of water from a flask and asked Sonny if he wanted some. Sonny declined.

"Tonight, we are to deliver two units. The first is here, and the other is about 10 kilometers away. But it seems we are early, or they are late," Henri mused with a troubled frown. "We have no choice but to wait."

Sonny glanced up at the stars in an alien sky. For the life of him, he couldn't remember what the stars and skies looked like that he and Raymond had stared at just about every night on their rooftop in New England. The clearing filled with men and women in berets and French Army attire—partisans.

"We were watching you, Henri," a woman spoke. "I can see that your protégé is used to the outdoors. I am impressed how this young man handled himself," she said.

Sonny countered, "They raised me in the woods."

The woman laughed. "Would you have seen us coming if you had you not been stargazing?"

The woman addressed Sonny in French. She was petite, with a cheerful grin and smiling brown eyes that peeked out from under her oversized beret. Sonny noted that she appeared to be in her late forties, dressed in black.

"I knew it was you, Madeleine," Henri said, giving her a hug.

"You're still alive, *mon ami*," she said.

"If we are to get these radios set up in your camp tonight, we should be off," Henri declared.

"*Si on allait se promener?*" she replied and motioned them to follow.

The moon that night, still oversized after the full moon the night before, was not the best for stealth. Madeleine instructed the group to stay on the sides of the path to prevent the moonlight from shining on them. She noted that Sonny had already been doing what she instructed.

Wolves raised him in his woods, Madeleine thought.

As they walked through the night, Madeleine locked eyes with the man she loved, knowing that their personal relationship would have to remain on hold as they devoted their energies to their mutual passion: to liberate their beloved France from Nazi occupation. Madeleine was divorced; Henri was a widower. *Perhaps, after the war, we could build a good life together in a new, free France.*

As they approached the main road, Madeleine motioned for the group to line up on the side to cross in unison. As they were about to cross, they heard shouting coming from the main road.

Madeleine directed the group to hide behind the hedgerow that lined the road.

***

Earlier that evening at the SS barracks, Sturmbannführer Gustav sat looking over deportment lists. His superiors were satisfied with his performance, but recent partisan activities were a thorn in his side. Something big was about to happen; he could sense it. He had met the Reichsführer of the Schutzstaffel, Heinrich Himmler, once, back in 1938. The Reichsführer had told him he had sensed his mystical powers when he was ordained into the ranks of the SS. When Germany invaded France in 1940, Gustav commanded an SS regiment. His tactical prowess earned him the Iron Cross. He had hoped to be part of the Russian campaign, but they denied his request to command on that front. Reichsführer Himmler instructed him to use his psychic powers to defeat the uprising in France, quell partisan activities, and restore order.

Madness, he thought. *I am better suited for front line combat, not this.*

Today he was drafting an order for the Jewish family of Maximilian and Rita Shemesh and their daughter Charlène to internment at the transit camp at Drancy, just northeast of Paris.

The Reichsführer was adamant about keeping precise records on the number of Jews deported. He hated this part of the job in France. Not that he didn't relish eliminating the Jewish population. He would rather lead his men in combat.

Disappointing, he thought. *Before I discovered Maximilian was a Jew, he was a* großartig *tailor! His wife Rita, although not of Jewish decent, was tainted by that* untermensch.

Gustav called for his orderly.

"Send a squad to arrest the Shemeshes," he said. "Take them to Drancy."

"*Jawohl!*" the orderly replied.

A Daughter's Revenge

Jack's parents' home was in the country. Houses lined both sides of the street, but several acres of land surrounded each house, so neighbors enjoyed the luxury of privacy. It was an established neighborhood, with mature trees and shrubs that felt like old friends to Jack, since they had grown up together. Now all he could think of was the horrific prospect of spies and snipers hiding behind those same trees and shrubs on his parent's estate.

I guess I got my adventure, Jack thought. *I would trade it all in a heartbeat to have my quiet life back.*

It was cloudy when Jack arrived at his father's house. When he left to return home at close to 6 p.m., it was drizzling. Jack turned on his wipers and kept them on all the way home as the drizzle gave way to a steady rain. He used his cell phone to call Emily at her office and on her cell phone, but both went to voicemail.

Weird, Jack thought, *I should reach her on one. She's must be in meetings. Emily's been working longer hours since her latest promotion; I almost never get to spend quality time with her anymore.*

Jack pulled up into their driveway, seeing Emily in the rain, holding an umbrella, leaning over to talk to a woman in a black sedan.

The rain was coming down harder and Jack parked the car to one side and ran towards Emily.

"I'd love to, let me just call Jack and check with him," he heard her say to the woman in the sedan, who he recognized in horror.

"Jack, nice to see you again! I was in town and wondered if you two would like to have dinner again. This time it's on me," Gisele said.

"It might be too late to get a table at our favorite place," Jack said, glancing at Emily.

"Oh, don't be silly, dear, they'll make room for us! As much time as we spend there, we could have a table inscribed with our names," Emily said.

Stay calm, stay calm, Jack thought. *I have to call Dad and Scotty to let them know the change in plans.*

"Come on, I'll drive," Gisele said motioning for them to get in her car.

"Sure, let's go dear," Emily chimed in.

"Let me shower first. I was working in the yard today," Jack said, stalling for time. "Emily, can you make drinks while I get cleaned up?"

"You look fine, but whatever works for you, dear," Emily answered. "Maybe I'll change into something more comfortable, like a sweatshirt and jeans."

Jack ran ahead in the rain to open the front door as Emily and Gisele strolled towards the car, sharing an umbrella, making small talk about Gisele's tour and Emily's work. Jack went into the master bedroom, feeling in his jeans for the cell phone his dad had given him. Patting his pant pockets in panic, Jack realized that the phone was still in his Durango. He was about to get it when Emily walked into the room.

"Hurry, dear," Emily said. "I just made 7 p.m. reservations for the three of us. We have less than an hour to get there."

"Sure, pick out some clothes for me, will you? I'll jump in the shower."

Damn it, thought Jack, *I need to get that phone. I should also tell Emily about Gisele. No, Emily might panic with Gisele in our house. I'll tell her after we get back from dinner.*

Jack showered and dressed in the clothes Emily had left for him on the bed. He put on his watch and put his cell phone in his shirt pocket and stood in front of his dresser, combing his hair.

"Geez, I hate this shirt," he said to himself, frowning. He removed the shirt and threw the offending object back on the bed. He reached in his closet for a shirt he liked better.

It only has a few wrinkles, so Emily won't scold, he thought as he tucked the shirt into his pants.

The women were conversing at the kitchen counter on bar stools when Jack walked in.

"Ready, dear?" Emily asked. She had changed into her favorite jeans and a sweatshirt that was a memento from their visit to Napa Valley.

"What, no drink for me?" Jack joked.

"We're late, let's go," Emily replied, motioning Jack and Gisele to the foyer.

Outside, Jack approached his Durango. "Should we take our car? That way if we stay out late, Gisele won't have to drive us all the way back here," he said.

Emily paused, agreeing with his logic, but Gisele interjected, "It's no inconvenience. My body clock doesn't know what time it's on because of my tour all over the map, so I'm happy to drive."

Jack was trapped. He reached for his own cell phone but realized he had left it in the shirt he had discarded in the house.

"Wait, I need my phone," Jack said as he bounded to his Durango. Emily started to protest, but Jack ignored her. He tried to open the passenger door, which stuck as usual. He jerked it open and grabbed the cell phone from the passenger seat.

"You should have that door fixed," Gisele commented as he jumped into the back seat, since Emily was already in the front passenger seat. The ride to the restaurant was only about 15 minutes and the ladies talked nonstop until they arrived.

Jack sat in the back, trying to figure out how and when he would be alone to call his dad and Scotty about the change in plans.

As they walked in, the restaurant owners approached Emily and Jack. They exchanged hugs, handshakes, and kisses.

Emily introduced Gisele to the owners, while Jack took their raincoats to the waiting room. A waitress escorted them to their favorite table.

After Jack had seated Gisele and Emily, he excused himself to use the restroom, reaching into his shirt pocket for the cell phone.

"Do you need your cell phone in the restroom, dear?" Emily asked, laughing.

"Force of habit, I guess," said Jack.

"Why, that's not even *your* cell phone," Emily commented, reaching for it. "Where did you get this antique contraption?"

Trapped, Jack stammered, "Oh, it's dad's. He let me borrow it till I have time to buy a new battery for my phone; mine doesn't seem to hold a charge anymore."

Emily rolled her eyes and shook her head, "You're getting expensive, mister," she said with a smirk, returning the phone to Jack.

Jack smiled and headed into the restroom. He locked the door, put down the toilet seat, flipped open the phone and dialed his parents' number.

His parents were talking with their British friends in the kitchen when the phone rang.

"Get that dear, my hands are wet," Claire commanded Joe.

"Sure, Queenie, anything for you," Joe replied.

"Hello," Joe said.

"Dad, it's me, Jack."

"I kind of figured that. What's up?"

"It's Gisele—she's with Emily and me at The High Tide, our favorite restaurant. When I got back from your house, she was parked in our driveway talking with Emily and she invited us to dinner." Jack's words came out in a rush.

"What's worse is we drove here in *her* car. Can you be here tonight? I'm so sorry, Dad. This all happened so fast I couldn't stop the ladies from arranging their impromptu rendezvous."

Joe interrupted, "Jack, calm down, we can be there within an hour. Do whatever you have to do to stall. Under no circumstances must you allow Gisele to leave the restaurant."

"Okay Dad, thanks." Jack blurted, "I'd better get back before Gisele suspects something."

"Good idea, Jack. Go back to dinner. Do your best to act normal and stall until we can get there." His dad signed off.

With her apron covered in flour and some unknown sauce, Claire announced that dinner was ready, only to see her husband and Scotty hobbling towards the front door, donning hats and coats as they left the house.

"I guess war heroes never retire," Claire said.

Back at The High Tide, Jack flushed the toilet in the restroom, just in case anyone was standing at the door listening. He washed his hands and combed his hair. He then set the cell phone to silent mode.

I don't want to tip Gisele off when Dad calls, he thought.

As he left the restroom, he blundered into a tall, muscular man with blond hair and a mustache.

"About time," the man muttered as he brushed rudely past Jack into the restroom, slamming the door behind him.

Jack felt a sharp pain in his left arm.

Damn impatient tourist, Jack thought, rubbing his arm.

"Act normal," Jack muttered to himself as he returned to the table.

"I've already been to the restroom and back and ordered a pint of your favorite beer. It's been sitting here getting warm," Emily teased.

"Not to worry, Jack, I was guarding it," said Gisele.

Jack took a sip. *I wonder if she tampered with my beer when Emily wasn't looking?*

Jack realized he was fidgeting too much. When they were waiting for their main course, and again after they had ordered dessert, Jack jumped up to go to the bar, on the pretext of checking on the game on the television in the bar area. There he checked the cell phone for any missed calls.

"Jack suffers from attention deficit disorder. That's why he can never sit still," Emily commented to Gisele.

Gisele giggled. "He does have a lot of energy. It's nice to see how devoted Jack is to you and his parents. From what he has said, they look out for Jack. I seldom witness that closeness among Americans," she commented.

"We are a close family," Emily agreed.

"I can't thank you both enough for introducing me to The High Tide," Gisele said when Jack returned from his third trip to the bar. "It's one of the best places I've been to. I must bring other friends here."

Not if I can help it, Jack thought.

When the check arrived, Jack looked around, hoping to see Scotty and his dad.

"Who are you looking for, dear?" Emily asked, startling Jack.

"Oh, just seeing if any of our neighbors are here tonight, but seems like it's packed with tourists this time of the year," Jack replied, turning red.

Just then the door swung open and Scotty stepped inside. He was wearing a tan raincoat and black bowler hat and tapped his cane as he approached the bar. All the patrons seated at the bar turned to stare at him.

Scotty strode up the bar and tapped his cane on the tile counter, declaring, "Barkeep! A gin and tonic, if you please."

Oh boy, thought Jack, *what is Scotty doing? Is this what he calls being unobtrusive?*

Gisele stared at the commotion Scotty was causing at the bar. "British people are so predictable, so pretentious—always strutting like peacocks," she said.

"But they are funny," Jack said.

He asked the women if they wanted another glass of wine. Gisele and Emily both nodded yes.

"They pack this place! I'll go up to the bar and get the wine," Jack said, grabbing their glasses.

Jack walked up to Scotty at the bar and whispered, "What are you doing? Every single person in here, including Gisele, noticed your grand entrance."

"No fear, my boy, I am just the decoy," Scotty replied, winking at Jack.

Jack shrugged. "I just wish you and Dad would have called me to tell me your plan, so I'd be better prepared," he grumbled, as he passed the empty wineglasses to the bartender.

"Where's Dad?" Jack asked. "Sonny's waiting in his car across the street," Scotty said, "ready for action."

Jack took the full wineglasses back to the table, glancing back with a grin at the sight of Scotty at the bar with his tan raincoat, bowler hat and cane.

Quite the decoy that Scotty is. He dominates the room like an elephant in a bathtub, Jack thought.

When they finished their wine, Emily declared it was time to call it a night.

"I have an early meeting tomorrow morning," she said, pushing her chair back.

As she stood up, Emily stumbled forward, knocking over the vase and the empty wine glasses on the table.

"Whoa, guess I had too much to drink," she mumbled.

"Maybe we should help her out," Gisele said to Jack.

"That's okay, I can get her," he said. But Jack was lightheaded, and his arm was numb, so he accepted Gisele's help, despite his reservations.

They flanked Emily, holding her by her waist as they walked out of the restaurant to the rear of the parking lot where Gisele had parked.

"Can you hold Emily for a minute while I open the passenger door for her?" he asked Gisele.

She nodded, and he walked to open the car door. When he looked up, he saw Emily slide from Gisele's grasp and drop to the ground. Jack raced around the car to rescue Emily.

He didn't get far. Jack's head exploded. A hard metal object smashed the right side of his face.

Jack's last view with his left eye as he fell to the ground was Gisele's tall legs in high-heeled shoes dragging an unconscious Emily into the back seat of her sedan.

Gisele opened the glove box, withdrew her grandfather's Walther PPK and screwed on the silencer. She walked to the rear of the sedan where Jack was lying face down in the mud, his hair matted with blood.

Just then, Scotty approached Gisele, lifting his bowler in acknowledgement. "It's good to see you again, Major Smythe," Gisele said to Scotty, hiding her PPK by her side.

"I wish I could say the same, but you deserve to join your grandfather in hell, Gisele," Scotty said with clenched teeth, taking in the sight of Jack lying motionless.

"My grandfather did not deserve to meet his maker with three hand grenades in his tunic," Gisele responded.

"The Butcher of Calais got what he deserved. I wish we could have done more to punish that madman," Scotty railed, pointing his cane at Gisele.

Gisele saw the barrel of the pistol concealed in Scotty's cane as he advanced towards Gisele. With greater speed and precision, she pulled the trigger, shooting Scotty twice, once in the head and once in the heart.

Gisele jumped into her sedan. She tossed her grandfather's still-smoking pistol on the front passenger seat. She careened onto the main road, with Emily flailing unconsciously in the back seat.

As Gisele's sedan raced past his parked car, Joe debated for a quick second to give chase, but he was transfixed by the figures lying in the restaurant parking lot.

"Please God, please God, no!" Joe cried as he turned his car and barreled into the restaurant parking lot.

Charlène

Henri spent much of the next day determining in whose care to place the nine-year-old Charlène to ensure the girl's safety. After much discussion, Antoinette selected a well-liked farming family in the town of Bergues and left the farmhouse to meet with them.

That evening, under the cover of dusk, Henri and Sonny took Charlène to the home of Pierre and Celeste Portiere, who had three children.

Sonny held Charlène's hand while she greeted the Portiere children, and Henri spoke to Pierre and Celeste, filling them in about the murder of Charlène's parents, killed by SS soldiers while trying to escape imprisonment at Drancy Interment camp.

"She is likely to have nightmares and may even be violent. I thank you both in advance for opening up your home to this orphan child and being gentle with her as she goes through the grieving process," he intoned.

"Our three children are friendly and boisterous, so they'll bring her out of her shell," Pierre offered. "We'll take good care of her and keep her active, so she does not dwell on unpleasant memories," Celeste promised.

"I'm sure that, as she heals, she will want to talk about her parents and her life, but until then, I've instructed our children not to pry," Celeste added.

Henri instructed that if anyone inquired about Charlène, the Portieres were to say she was Celeste's niece visiting from Paris; Celeste's sister- and brother-in-law sent their nine-year-old daughter to live with her aunt and family in the country.

Sonny and Henri hugged Charlène goodbye. She clung to Sonny's leg, begging him to stay with her. Sonny pleaded with Henri to take her back with them to the farmhouse, but Henri would not budge.

"They will look for her, and someone will notice her at the farmhouse. I hope that because the Portieres have three children, she'll blend in there with no one becoming too curious."

Sonny promised he would visit Charlène as much as possible without calling attention to her whereabouts. He dried her tears with his handkerchief and gave her his beret as a present. It covered most of her face, but she pushed back the beret and smiled with her brown eyes.

As Sonny and Henri left the house, Charlène reached for Celeste's hand, and they walked back to the kitchen.

Celeste made hot chocolate with homemade whipping cream for the children. Charlène sipped at hers while the other three gulped theirs and ran into the parlor.

Celeste escorted Charlène to the parlor after she had finished her hot chocolate. There they watched Caryll practicing on the piano, and Andre and Francesca playing checkers, until Celeste announced it was time for the children to prepare for bed.

Caryll and Francesca shared a room upstairs. Pierre brought a mattress from Andre's room and placed it on the floor between the girl's beds for Charlène to sleep. Celeste made up the bed and left the room, returning with a pale blue nightgown, four dresses, and several pairs of socks, which she placed on the dresser. She placed a pair of brown shoes and soft white slippers for Charlène in the closet.

Francesca introduced Charlène to her dolls and Caryll shared her book collection. Andre came in to show Charlène his new soccer ball. The three siblings jabbered away at their new young houseguest, who listened to their stories, but said nothing.

At about 9 p.m., Charlène excused herself to use the bathroom and change into her nightgown. She returned, holding her dirty clothes in a pile in her small hands and stood in the doorway, unsure what to do next.

Celeste smiled with pride as her daughter Caryll jumped up from her bed and sat on Charlène's bed. "Charlène, I love sleeping on the floor, so why don't you have my bed?"

Celeste shut the door to her daughter's room and went downstairs to sit with her husband in the parlor.

"That child will come around, Pierre. Charlène's a survivor, and our girls are showing her a lot of affection," she said.

Charlène thanked Caryll for her generosity and climbed into her bed. She listened to the two girls saying their night prayers and calling out goodnight to their parents and brother. She mumbled goodnight to both of them as she stifled another yawn.

Within minutes, Charlène was fast asleep.

Celeste took Charlène's clothes downstairs and was about to throw them into the rubbish bin in the kitchen when she reconsidered. *I think I'll wash them and save them for Charlène. Poor child, these clothes are all she has left of her past*, Celeste thought.

Charlène awoke at 6 a.m. the next morning to the smell of baked croissants and strong coffee. She washed up and dressed in the bathroom and ventured down the stairs into the kitchen.

She saw Pierre sitting at a table reading a newspaper and Celeste cutting fruit for a salad. Pierre pulled out a chair for Charlène and Celeste placed a croissant and a glass of milk in front of her.

"The quiche is in the oven and I'll serve it when our lazy children wake up in the next hour," she said. "We will have trouble when they have to get up early when school resumes."

Charlène devoured her meal as if she hadn't eaten in days. She ate the second croissant Celeste put on her plate without hesitation.

Pierre looked up from behind his newspaper and smiled. *A strong appetite is a good sign,* he thought.

He announced that he would feed the chickens and collect eggs and invited Charlène along. She accepted the basket Celeste offered to her. Putting on the shoes she had set by the door, Charlène followed Pierre to the chicken coops. Trailing them was Simon, the family terrier.

Pierre showed Charlène how to sprinkle meal in the far corners of the penned areas to keep the roosters from fighting over their food. When he saw that they had distributed the food, he let the chickens out of the coops and showed Charlène which bowls to fill.

Pierre then showed her how to reach into the coops and collect eggs, one by one. He watched her progress and helped her stack the eggs in the basket. About 40 minutes later, the basket was full, and Pierre picked it up and said it was time to return to the farmhouse for breakfast.

Charlène lagged, stopping to stare at the little chicks that were picking at the ground in a fenced area next to the coops, chuckling at a black and red rooster that was poaching on a competitor's meal, and surveying brown fields that stretched for what seemed like miles.

Henri was right, this child has never been in a farm environment before, Pierre thought. *Perhaps she'll feel like she's on a new adventure and she'll not dwell on the horror of watching her parents killed. It will be nice to see her happy.*

Celeste called to them to wash up and join the others in the kitchen for breakfast. Charlène ate a quiche, warm smoked sausages, and fresh fruit. She listened to the talk at the table but again she didn't join in the conversations.

After breakfast, she skipped rope with Francesca in front of the house and then took Simon for a walk through the farm to a small stream where Francesca said her father and Andre had

111

taught her how to fish. Then they spent two hours throwing sticks to Simon, who raced and retrieved them until the girls were too tired to throw another stick.

They returned to the house, flushed and satisfied. They giggled when they saw that Simon had beaten them to the house, but had fallen asleep with exhaustion, sunbathing on the porch.

Celeste provided each of the girls a pastry and hot chocolate. After their snack, Charlène sat down in a comfortable high-back chair in the parlor with a book Caryll provided before she returned to piano practice.

Charlène dozed off and woke up by Francesca shaking her, announcing that lunch was ready. Lunch was a thick beef stew served with mini baguettes, home churned butter, and hot apple cider.

After lunch, the children played outside until Celeste called them in to clean up and take an afternoon nap.

At 6 p.m. that evening, Charlène awakened to the sound of a radio playing. Careful not to wake her two new friends and roommates, she tip-toed downstairs and found Celeste and Pierre in the parlor, listening to guttural German announcements about recent victories and "much progress made to eradicate filthy Jews."

When they saw Charlène standing wide-eyed and scared in the doorway, Pierre turned the radio off and Celeste rushed to comfort the girl, who shaked and sobbed.

"We hid from those monsters for five days, but they hunted us down and killed my parents," Charlène said. "Sonny saved me. If it wasn't for Sonny, I'd be dead too."

Celeste picked Charlène up in her arms and cradled the young girl in her lap in an oversized chair in the parlor. She rocked Charlène to sleep singing her children's favorite lullaby.

When Charlène awoke again in the parlor, it was dark outside and there were excited voices coming from the kitchen, along with the savory smell of roasted chicken and rosemary.

She feasted with the Portiere family on chicken, baby potatoes and beans, accompanied by warm multi-grain bread and milk.

After dinner, they retired to the parlor to listen to Caryll playing classical favorites until it was time for bed.

Celeste tucked the girls in and smiled as her daughters attempted to draw Charlène out of her shell with jokes and laughter.

She heard Charlène giggle at one of Francesca's jokes.

I'm glad she is at least feeling comfortable with us, Celeste thought. *She'll soon share her history with us as soon as she feels she can trust us. I would love to know more about this sweet child—her favorite foods, her hobbies, what was her routine in her family life?*

During the following weeks, Charlène blossomed under the loving care and parenting of Pierre and Celeste, the sincere friendship their children offered to her, and the day-to-day peaceful routine they helped her create as part of their family on a busy farm.

The Portieres learned that Charlène spoke three languages. She read and wrote fluent English, Italian, and French. She was a gifted pianist, an amateur chess champion, and an expert seamstress. All this accomplishment at age nine!

She told the Portieres that her father, Maximilian Shemesh, was a tailor by trade and that her mother, Rita, was a famous chef who ran a patisserie in Versailles and who worked part time at the library because she loved books and history. They lived above the brick building that housed her father's tailor shop and her mother's bakery and café.

Charlène said she had attended the local convent school until the Germans had bombed it. "After that, my mother stopped working at the library so she could tutor me at home," Charlène said.

"My parents rarely spoke about their own parents," Charlène said. "I once overheard my mother telling a friend she hadn't seen her parents since she eloped with my father twelve years ago. My father once told me his parents died in Poland and that he had a brother who went to America before the war and now lived on a farm in Virginia."

Charlène told the Portieres that her family had fled Versailles in the back of a run-down truck five weeks before she came to live with them. "My father made stylish wool and silk suits for Manon Vuitton, our local banker. He came to our home one night and handed my father a list with his name and my name on it. Mr. Vuitton said the Germans were rounding up Jewish families and taking them away in trucks, wagons, and trains, and that we should leave.

My parents said that the Nazis didn't care that my mother was French. Because my father was Jewish, they would take me to concentration camps with other Jewish children and put us to death.

They spirited away us in a truck to Saint-Omer, where Jacqueline Boudreau, a friend my mother had known since culinary school, hid us for five nights in her home. We all thought we were safe..." said Charlène, her voice trailing away.

Celeste and Pierre said nothing, waiting for Charlène to continue her story when she was ready.

"The local butcher joked to an undercover Gestapo agent, who was in his shop, that Jacqueline must feed another entire family because she had more than doubled her standing meat order during the past week," Charlène explained.

"Jacqueline's husband Jacques was told the SS were coming to take us away, so he drove us to the outskirts of their town after dark and dropped us off on a dirt road. He told us to walk east for seven miles to the next town. He gave my mother an envelope with a letter addressed to a friend who would take us in, with his name and address written on the front. But just ten minutes after we began walking, the SS were upon us. They shot my father in the back. I turned around to see how many enemies there were, but it was too dark. I remember screaming.

My mother fell down on her knees and held me close. She made me promise that I'd stay calm. 'You must live,' she kept telling me, over and over, holding my face in her hands and crying. She told me to run to the left and that she would run to the right to distract the SS. 'Remember I love you, always,' were her last words to me," Charlène said, sobbing.

"I ran into the bushes and a young man caught me. I scratched him and bit him because I thought he was the enemy, but he held me tight and told me he would take care of me. When the Nazis shot and killed my mother, he sang a song to me, like my mother used to do. I couldn't stop crying. Sonny kept his word. He kept me safe."

"I feel safe with you also," she said to Celeste and Pierre. "Thank you for letting me join your family," she said, sitting at their feet. Celeste pulled her up and hugged her close. "We are your family, child, and we will always be," she told Charlène.

When the family went into town, they often confronted curiosity about Charlène. Whether at the hardware store, local market or the park, local Nazi sympathizers and Gestapo often stopped to ask questions about Charlène. She bore no resemblance to Celeste, so some gossiped about whether she was Celeste's niece.

Sonny came to visit Charlène about three days a week, bringing her a teddy bear, books, and painting supplies. Sonny often joined the Portieres for dinner and regaled the family with stories about growing up near a farm in America.

This was a busy time for the French Resistance; rumors of an impending Allied invasion of the French coast were rampant. Henri was cautious since the Germans listened to the same rumors. They had stepped up their land and sea patrols attempting to quiet partisan activity.

It was warmer, which reminded Sonny of the days he sprinted out of high school in early spring, his jacket unbuttoned but still kept on for warmth from the spring chill. He pulled off his watch cap, a black wool knit cap donned by most of the men in his group, to wipe his brow. The hidden cave they were in was dusty and musty, but he had to continue to assemble the radios that the Operation Jedburgh teams would take with them.

Preparations for the invasion were comprised of fake radio transmissions in a code that the German intelligence cracked, supporting Operation Fortitude, the fake invasion of Pas-de-Calais. Elements of the German 15th Army had occupied the area, so the partisans had to coordinate their missions and execute them. A single misstep meant torture and death.

Around this time, an SS-Sturmbannführer, a ranking officer, and SS-Oberscharführer, a senior enlisted soldier, appeared each night at the local inn, a quaint country bistro and pension just a stone's throw from Henri's farmhouse, which made operations in the hidden cave much more difficult.

Henri and his team discussed moving their radio building operation but concurred that it would be perilous to move now, with the countryside teeming with German soldiers and spies. So, the partisans developed a system of couriers and signals to alert their colleagues to the approach of Germans.

One day, while Sonny was eating lunch at the inn, he looked up to see the Oberscharführer, who had ordered Charlène's family taken to Drancy, come in for a mid-day meal. He entered the dining room, followed by another officer, a Sturmbannführer. *He appears uneasy as he looks around,* Sonny thought.

A fork could have cut the tension building in the air, until Françoise, the innkeeper deflated it by saying: "Gentlemen, welcome to my inn, would you like a glass of local red wine and some savory beef stew?"

The Oberscharführer replied "At once!" as he and the Sturmbannführer sat down at a corner table facing the interior, their backs to the wall.

Sonny blended in and buried his face in his stew, sipping on a glass of red wine. As the SS soldiers waited for their meal, the Sturmbannführer stood up and walked towards Sonny.

"How's the stew?" he asked Sonny in French.

"*Très bon,*" Sonny replied. "Françoise makes it with the finest beef in all of France."

"Maybe you can tell me some interesting places for me to see in this area," the Sturmbannführer said. "What is your name?"

"Sonny," came the nervous reply. "Have I done something wrong?"

"No," the Sturmbannführer replied, "But it seems odd that a young man like you is taking his afternoon meal alone. One would think you would ready the fields for planting or dressing the catch of the day by the docks."

Sonny was about to answer, but he panicked. His face turned red as he stammered. The Sturmbannführer crossed his arms and stared at Sonny's discomfort.

Just then, Henri burst into the inn, yelling at Sonny: "Boy! So, this is where you vanished. We haven't finished cleaning the fishing boat; leave it to you to abandon the rest of us for food!"

He looked from Sonny to the Sturmbannführer, then grabbed Sonny by the arm and dragged him away.

"We have other business to attend to today, so go clean your boat, Sonny," the Sturmbannführer said to the departing men.

The Sturmbannführer sat down, sipped his wine and moments later made satisfied grunting sounds as he slurped the beef stew.

Outside the inn, Henri released Sonny, smoothing out his shirt.

"We had been warned by MI-6 that the SS pulled into the area this morning, Sonny. We should stay close the farmhouse to avoid raising their suspicions. Their patrols are combing the countryside. You should also stay away from the Portieres. My hunch is that they are hunting Charlène."

"Have we another safe place for Charlène to go, Henri?"

"That we do, *mon ami*, that we do," Henri replied as they walked back to the fishing boat.

Later that day the children were kicking Andre's soccer ball around in the field behind the farmhouse when Simon began barking, alerting them to a truck pulling up to the front of the house. They stopped playing and started to walk towards the house when two SS burst through the front door.

The children joined hands and listened. They held their breath as a scuffle ensued inside. Overhead, bluebirds chirped, unaware of the tension on the ground.

A few minutes later the back door opened and Celeste, with an ashen face consumed with fear, called: "Charlène, come inside, my darling, there are two soldiers here who would like to speak with you."

Charlène stiffened. Pleading with Caryll and Francesca to loosen their tight grip on her hands, she walked into the house, tears beading up in her eyes.

The other three children stood paralyzed. Only Simon's barking and the bluebirds chirping broke the silence outside the house. Inside the house, yelling, threats and the sound of broken glass gave way to screams and then silence.

About an hour later, the three children raced into the house with the dog, unprepared for the horror within.

At 8 p.m., as Henri smoked his pipe in the study, he received an urgent handwritten note delivered by the stable boy:

Come now! It is Charlène.

Henri's eyeglasses fell onto his chair. He dropped his pipe in the bowl and his Cognac glass knocked to the floor. "*Mon Dieu, mon Dieu,*" he said as he jumped up and called to Sonny.

Henri and Sonny entered through the Portieres back door. Celeste sobbed at her kitchen table, as Pierre grasped her in a hug to keep her from falling.

"I couldn't do anything to protect her," she choked out through her sobs. "Those monsters tortured our little darling while they pinned me to the floor. They put a gun to my head."

Sonny's entire body turned icy, as if all the blood had flowed out of his body. He and Henri rushed upstairs to find Charlène in a small bed, her face so swollen and bruised she was unrecognizable.

Pierre said, "They came when I was tilling the fields beyond view of the farmhouse. They hit Celeste with a gun, tied her mouth and hands, and threw her on the floor while they interrogated and tortured Charlène. They broke the child's leg, her arm, and they hit her face and head with a rifle butt."

Celeste came upstairs and pushed back the hair, matted in blood, framing Charlène's face.

"I tried to scream for them to stop through the handkerchief they had pushed into my mouth, but they would not stop," Celeste said, whimpering as she recollected the horror of that afternoon.

Sonny approached Charlène, wondering if she was dead.

She stirred, opening her right eye to see who was in the room. Her left eye was swollen, and her face and lips cut and discolored. Sonny ran to her side and grasped her hand. She winced in pain, so he relaxed his grip.

"*Ça va?*" he asked.

"*Ils m'ont fait mal,*" Charlène replied.

Since they had rescued Charlène after they gunned her parents down, Sonny had grown fond of the frail girl with curly brown hair and a shy smile. He had enjoyed visiting her and looked forward to his visits with the Portiere family who had taken her in.

Now he wondered if this was his fault: *had the Gestapo watched his visits all along?* The thought tore at his sanity.

Charlène whispered to him, trying to sit up before she fell unconscious, "Sonny, *Je n'ai rien dit, je n'ai rien dit…*"

Sonny turned to Pierre and asked, "I didn't say anything?"

"An officer and a soldier wearing the SS insignias were asking around the village if anyone had information about the attacks on German soldiers a few weeks ago. Someone must have told them they thought Charlène was at the site of the killings. They came here looking for our children's cousin. They tortured Charlène to extract the names of those who killed the SS soldiers, but she did not say a word, brave child!" Pierre said.

Pierre broke down into sobs, holding Celeste close.

As the night wore on, Sonny continued to hold Charlène's hand. Several times, Henri insisted that they must leave before the SS soldiers came back, but Sonny refused to leave Charlène's side.

With much trepidation, Henri left Sonny at the house.

"Be careful. If they return, you must say you are a friend of the family. I fear you are at risk being caught, but I understand, Sonny."

Henri slipped out the back door.

Charlène awoke a few times during the night, each time reaching for Sonny's hand and saying, "Sonny, *je ne dis pas, je ne dis pas.*"

A local doctor Pierre had summoned came to check on Charlène. She appeared agitated as he checked her wounds. Sonny remembered the song he had concocted to soothe Charlène after she had witnessed her parents' murders. It was her favorite: "Lili Marlene."

Sonny cried as he stroked Charlène's matted hair and sang to her until she drifted off again into unconsciousness.

He had failed to take care of Charlène. They had hurt the innocent little girl. Sonny sat in the chair by Charlène's bed as he plotted revenge. At 4 a.m., Pierre summoned Sonny to follow him downstairs. A truck with SS had pulled into the inn's parking lot before midnight.

"You must go to the farmhouse and hide, Sonny!" Pierre implored. Sonny agreed and slipped out the back door of the Portiere's farmhouse.

The next morning, as the team sat in the study with their coffee, a wagon carrying a wooden coffin pulled up at the Portiere's farmhouse after dawn.

Hunter or Hunted?

Jack awoke to his head throbbing and the taste of warm blood in his mouth. His right eye was swollen shut. His head hurt to the touch and his left arm was numb, but he used his right arm to propel himself into a sitting position. He looked around. That's when he saw Scotty's body, lying crumbled on the ground, his cane a few feet away and his bowler hat in the bushes.

Emily, he thought, *that damn Gisele took Emily*.

Jack fought back tears. "Gisele better not harm Emily," he muttered.

Jack staggered to his feet and walked to Scotty. He sat by Scotty, softly shaking him. He was still groggy.

"Scotty wake up."

It confused me even before Gisele ambushed me and hit me in the face with her gun, he thought. He reached into his coat pocket and found Joe's cell phone. *Thank God Gisele hadn't taken it*.

He was lucky he wasn't dead, but he had to wonder: *Why didn't she just kill me? She could have done so*. His disjointed thoughts came together, fitting like a puzzle: *Gisele left me alive because Scotty intervened. She killed Scotty in cold blood and kidnapped Emily. But Emily and I are insignificant in Gisele's twisted mind, pawns. She's hunting World War II veterans. She got Scotty and now she's hunting Dad.*

Jack surveyed the parking lot, wondering if there were any patrons leaving the restaurant to which he could yell for help. That's when he saw his dad's car at the opposite end of the parking lot. He watched his dad lift Scotty's body into the back seat. Joe then walked up to Scotty's car, looking in the back seat for something.

From the back porch of the restaurant, Jack yelled out to his dad, but Joe had hearing problems and did not hear him at first. Jack mustered all the strength he could and whistled, yelling out, "Dad, I'm over here!"

Joe saw his son hunched on the porch steps. He ran over to Jack and picked him up with surprising strength. Jack leaned on Sonny as they walked to his car, and Sonny strapped Jack into the front passenger seat.

Holding up Jack's chin, Joe wiped the blood, tears, mud, and grime from his son's face. Jack winced when his father patted his head.

"Pistol whipped you, did she?" he asked. Jack nodded.

Joe asked, "Did Gisele take Emily?" Jack nodded again, unable to speak. Tears and blood continued to roll down his face.

"We will get Emily back, son; I promise," Joe vowed.

"How? Gisele always seems to be one step ahead of us," Jack said, choking back more tears.

"Next time we'll do this right, but first we have to take Scotty's body back to the house. I have to make some phone calls. Don't tell anyone about this; Gisele might harm Emily," Joe cautioned.

"Dad, I'm afraid. I can't bear the thought of losing Emily," Jack said. His tears welled up again.

"Don't worry; as long as I'm alive, I promise we'll get Emily back in one piece," Joe promised.

Joe drove Jack to the local 24-hour emergency clinic. The clinic treated Jack's head wound and checked to see if he had sustained broken bones or other internal injuries. He left the clinic with nine stitches above his right eye. Joe lied that Jack had too much to drink and fell face first in the bar's parking lot.

They then drove home, where Joe broke the bad news to Trudy. Claire brought Trudy a sedative and sat with her on the couch until she fell asleep. Jack had gone to bed in his old room and plunged into a deep, painkiller induced sleep. He had on muddied clothes on top of the covers and was sleeping with all the lights on when his parents walked in to check on him.

Claire laid a quilt over her son. They turned off the lights and went downstairs to sit with the sedated widow of the war hero Scotty Smythe.

Early the next morning, a gray Ford cargo van bearing the name of a local dry cleaner came to the house. Two men got out and spoke with Joe.

Joe left his family to go open the garage door. The two men entered the garage, putting on gloves. One of them carried a large black bag. They put Scotty's body into the bag and loaded it into the back of the cargo van. One man then asked Joe for his car keys. The men left, one driving the cargo van they came in and the other driving Joe's car, heading to the "cleaners."

That afternoon, Jack awoke in his old bedroom, still stiff and sore. His mouth was dry, and he had a high fever. He got out of bed and went into the bathroom.

"I look like I've been in a war," he said to his reflection in the medicine cabinet mirror. His right eye was swollen shut and the back of his head hurt like hell. His mother came into the bedroom, placing a pitcher of ice water, a glass, and two aspirin, by his bed. She instructed him to take the pills and return to bed.

After dinner, Joe entered Jack's room just as he was stirring. "How are you feeling?"

"Like a Mack truck hit me," Jack said. "Any word from Gisele?"

"No," Sonny replied, "I suspect she has some misguided idea about displaying honor by giving us a day or two to take care of Scotty's burial before she strikes again. While there's no doubt she's hunting me, I'd bet my last dollar her demented mind is waiting for just the right moment to take me out."

"I'm terrified for Emily, Dad! It's all my fault. I should have warned her," Jack said sobbing.

"Don't worry, Emily will be fine, like I said, it's me Gisele wants. I'm sure she'll agree to a swap: me for Emily," Joe said.

"No way, Dad! I can't let you do that. We have to call the FBI and get them to help us," Jack shouted. His head ached as his voice echoed over and over.

"We have no choice; we can't involve the authorities. I'll make sure that if I go, Gisele goes too. But first I have to make sure Emily is safe," Joe said. "Besides, I'm an old man. I've lived a long, happy life with a wife I adore and a son I'm proud of."

"Now get some rest!" Joe ordered, covering Jack with the quilt Claire had used the night before. "I think your fever has broken."

Jack drifted off to sleep as his father got up from the side of his bed and left the room.

Sturmbannführer Fredrik Gustav served in the SS Adolf Hitler Division during World War II. Partisans killed him in 1944 in the little French town of Bergues. His wife had died of typhoid when she was twenty-eight, and Gustav had raised his daughter, Ingrid, alone. They alternated their roles as caregivers to each other. When Ingrid married wealthy steel mill owner Rolf Toffler, Fredrik Gustav moved in with them to their country estate in the little town of Augsburg in Bavaria.

Ingrid never recovered from her father's death. To make matters worse, the Toffler's firstborn, they diagnosed a son Erik with polio when he was two and died at age six. In 1962, three months before Gisele was born, Rolf died in a freak hunting accident in the Bavarian forest. The family suspected another assassination took place.

Gisele inherited her mother's hatred for Fredrik's assassins. Ingrid regaled Gisele with stories of Fredrik's heroism and the many enemies of the Third Reich whom he had killed, prior to his own death by partisans in 1944.

After her mother died after a long battle with cancer in 1997, Gisele was 35, single and alone. Tall and striking with long blond hair, icy cold blue eyes, and a slim, shapely figure, she was a perfect Aryan specimen.

In 1999, Gisele flew from Frankfurt to New York. She rented a car and drove through the city and various surrounding neighborhoods. Within two weeks, she rented two homes. The first was a small rundown house in a poor part of a small town, near Newark, where teenage boys hanging around their front porches across the street whistled at her. But no one approached her front door.

Gisele's second rental was a quaint cottage on a quiet lane in the Hamptons. There were five other homes on her lane, and after Gisele first moved in, various neighbors stopped by. They brought wine, caviar and flowers to welcome her to the neighborhood.

But Gisele never answered her door. She stood at an upstairs window, peering from behind her lace curtains until she saw them drive or walk away, leaving their gifts with a note on her front porch.

"Stupid, meddlesome Americans," Gisele muttered. "They should spend time with their own families, not come over to their neighbor's homes unannounced without being invited."

When she walked back into the library in her home, where she spent every waking moment poring over her grandfather's journals, Gisele always stopped at the fireplace mantle to kiss the photo of her mother Ingrid and her grandfather Fredrik.

Consumed by hate for the Allies who had destroyed her grandfather, Gisele spent countless hours in various public libraries, wading through stacks of declassified documents about American World War II veterans who served behind enemy lines in France and Germany.

She conducted searches on her laptop online, typing the names of World War II veterans she identified as targets. Gisele vowed that she would hunt down each one of them, exacting revenge for robbing her mother of her father, and Gisele of her grandfather.

Gisele devised a clever way to get close to her grandfather's enemies. She visited them on the pretext of doing research for a book and a video about their exploits. Gisele's beauty and interest charmed many of those she interviewed. They spent hours with her, telling lengthy stories with vivid details about their missions during World War II.

Gisele left her house in the Hamptons in a rental car, a dark green Chevy Malibu, and drove to her run-down house in New Jersey. She parked across the street and began walking, much to the delight of three teenage boys who emitted a series of wolf whistles as she walked past them.

"Hey baby, good to see you again," one of them said to Gisele.

"Shut up, Tom, leave the lady alone. It's not like you haven't seen her," his friend remarked. "She was at the house yesterday and I saw her three times last week."

Gisele smiled at the boys and walked up to her house.

Upon entering, Gisele checked to make sure she locked the front door. She lowered the blinds and turned on a hallway light. She then opened the door to the basement and ambled down the stairs.

Emily awoke and looked around to get her bearings. She appeared to be in a basement area, the floor was cement and there was a little office setup in the corner. She was bound to a hard, wooden chair and her mouth was held shut with duct tape.

Emily's eyes opened wide with terror as she saw Gisele come to stand over her, pinching Emily's face into a pout with her left hand. In her right hand, Gisele held a dark silver pistol, onto which Gisele screwed a silencer.

"Don't worry, my dear Emily, I will not kill you, at least not yet anyway," Gisele said, rubbing the pistol against Emily's hair.

She sashayed in front of Emily, holding out the pistol in the palms of her hands, mimicking how a sommelier presents an expensive bottle of wine to her host.

"This was my grandfather's favorite pistol, and he would be proud of what I've accomplished with it during the past two years," Gisele crowed.

"If you promise not to scream, I will take off the duct tape," she said pointing her gun at Emily. "But if you scream, you will die, understand?"

Emily nodded her head, as the tears that formed in her eyes ran down her cheek.

Emily winced as Gisele ripped the tape from her mouth.

"Why are you doing this?" Emily asked Gisele, defeated, sure she would die.

Gisele snorted in derision. "I thought it would be obvious to you, but your husband Jack kept you in the dark about my quest for justice, Fraulein."

"My grandfather was Sturmbannführer Frederik Gustav," Gisele declared. "He was a decorated officer who served Germany under a great leader. Your father-in-law and his friends murdered my grandfather. They took his life in a sadistic and evil manner.

It's your father-in-law I'm after, or should I say, I will not rest until I kill a certain Allied Operative whose code name was Sonny," Gisele disclosed. "Sonny's death must be painful and gruesome, because that is what my grandfather would have wished," Gisele said, opening a crate that contained World War II-style pineapple hand grenades.

"Your grandfather served Hitler?" Emily asked. "Are you calling that madman a great leader?" she asked, horrified. Gisele slapped Emily's face with the butt of the Walther PPK. It was a stinging pain, followed by the warm taste of salty blood.

Gisele droned on as if delivering a speech: "I have ferreted out each one of my grandfather's murderers and punished them. Only Code Name Sonny remains. I'm saving the best for last."

Gisele grabbed the roll of duct tape again and encircled it around Emily's mouth and hair, making her eyes well with tears from the excruciating pain. "Tomorrow," she said in a fierce whisper in Emily's ear, "I will eradicate Code Name Sonny with extreme prejudice."

Gisele pulled out a small bottle and syringe from a nearby desk. She drew some clear liquid as Emily waited, fearing to breathe.

"Don't worry Emily," Gisele said as she inserted the needle in the carotid artery in Emily's neck, "I need you alive for now."

Emily struggled to avoid the needle, but her efforts were futile, since she was pinned in the chair. As she succumbed to the sedation and drifted off to sleep, she listened to a door close and a bolt slide into place.

Three days had passed, and Jack was beyond frantic with worry over Emily. At 11:18 a.m. on the fourth morning, the phone rang. He overheard his father say to the caller, "If you don't let Emily go, there is no place on this planet you can hide where I will not hunt you down and kill you."

He paused for a moment and then responded to the caller: "Yes, I know the place. I'll be there at nine." Sonny, walked into the room where Jack was recovering, "She wants to meet me tonight at nine o'clock and she will bring Emily."

"Dad, I want to go, you can't do this alone. And she has my wife," Jack pleaded.

"No, you're still hurt, and you'll only get in the way. I can handle her myself. I need to make sure first that Emily is safe. If only Scotty were here," Joe said.

"But Dad—" Jack begged again.

"No," Joe said. "I need you to watch your mother. Get the shotgun out of the study and go to the basement and lock the door. Do not answer the phone and do not open the door for anyone until I get back," Joe directed. "Got it?"

"All right, I will," said Jack. "Careful, Dad. I want you both home; alive and well."

"Will do," Joe said.

Joe was ready to go when Claire came in, giving him a bear hug and kissing him goodbye. He handed his wife a folded sheet of paper, which she tucked into her apron.

"Have some coffee ready for me when I get back, Queenie, I'll need it," Joe said as he left.

"Dear. Don't get back too late, okay?" Claire responded.

Claire walked to the car with her husband and held his door open as he got in and drove away, waving to her as he left. She walked back to the house and closed the door, with tears running down her face.

"Don't worry Mom. Dad knows what he is doing," Jack offered.

"That's the problem, Jack," his mother said, smiling, but said no more.

Jack pulled the shotgun and a box of shells from a metal lockbox in the study. His mother had blankets and pillows in her arms as they descended to the basement.

The two sat on the floor. Neither spoke as about 30 minutes passed. Glass broke somewhere above them. Must be the window in the den, he guessed. Jack rose, intent on walking towards the steps to look more and listen. But his mother held him back, whispering, "Jack, don't go upstairs; remember what your father said."

"Okay," he whispered and walked to the end table to pick up the shotgun. Grabbing two shells, he prepared to load them into the shotgun when the door to the basement opened and the light clicked on.

"Dad?" Jack asked, walking towards the stairs. He then began to retreat as he saw a pair of heavy military-style black boots descending the stairs. The two shells fell to the ground.

"No," was the response from a tall muscular blonde man, who Jack recognized: the man who had collided with him at the restaurant.

The man approached Claire, brandishing an ominous military style knife in his right hand.

So, Gisele is not working solo, Jack thought. "Dammit, what is Dad walking into," he said aloud in horror.

"I don't think you will see Dad again," the tourist from The High Tide said.

Jack did not hesitate. He cocked the shotgun and pointed it at the man. He pulled the trigger, click.

"Crap! I forgot to load the shotgun," Jack said.

The intruder leaped at Jack, knocking him to the ground. Jack fought back but was overpowered. Jack started to pass out from the chokehold of the German's hands circling his neck. Just as he pulled the knife up high to make a downward stroke at his chest, the resounding boom of pistol fire echoed in the basement.

He then blacked out. Jack didn't know how long he remained unconscious. When he awoke, Claire had covered him with a blanket. A pillow under his head. His mother sat in a chair beside his makeshift bed, fidgeting with her apron.

"What happened?" he asked his mother.

"Your father isn't the only one good with a gun, Jack. Never underestimate a woman, or you'll end up like him," she said pointing to the body near the stairs.

"I'll say," Jack replied as he saw the tourist lying dead against one wall of the basement with a bullet hole drilled into his temple. There were bloody marks across the floor, marking the path where his mother had dragged the body.

"What about Dad?" Jack asked. "He never told me where he was going."

"He told *me*," Claire said, as she took out the folded note from her apron. Blood and flour covered the note.

The Raid

As rumors of an impending Allied invasion grew daily, Sonny was busy repairing radios and distributing the units around the vicinity of Pas-de-Calais. Marie and Sergio carried out bogus radio transmissions to keep the Germans focused on the wrong target. It was dangerous work, as German troops continued to pour into the area.

Little Charlène always came to Sonny's mind. Anger boiling within him at the Nazis' cruel torture of an innocent child. Henri fretted over Sonny's pensive grief. Henri tried to keep Sonny busy, assigning him various chores to occupy his time: cleaning the stables, feeding the chickens and pigs, and herding the sheep. He commiserated with Sonny's sadness about what had happened to Charlène. But Henri steadfast in his focus: their mission was to annihilate the Nazis. Along the way, they would all lose family, friends, and fellow partisans, and see many innocent people die.

"The innocents who are casualties of war are most unfortunate, but they are a sad reality in this mad world," Henri would tell the team.

Sonny smiled when he received word that they would fly a Jedburgh team in to assist in an air raid.

Could this be the long-awaited invasion to liberate France? Is it going to happen, Sonny thought?

Most of what Sonny had experienced so far was death, dying, brutality, and destruction. He longed for the war to be over, for freedom, for home.

Henri called a meeting for that evening.

"We set a nighttime air raid on May 23rd, 1944 to disrupt SS activity in the area," Henri said.

"What is the target," Sergio asked.

"The SS barracks and nearby marshaling grounds. A British de Havilland DH.98 Mosquito bomber group, flown by Polish pilots will fly the raid. They seek retribution for the Nazi massacre of their country's men, women, and children."

After a few days of patrolling the area with the Free French partisans, the Jedburgh team felt the time was right to begin their operation. Outfitted with Sonny's radios, civilian clothes, and paired up with local partisans, they set up watch positions near the SS compound.

After supper, Henri called Marie and Sergio to the library to discuss their part in the operation. He asked Antoinette to summon Sonny from the cave.

"I want you to be with us on this one," Henri said to Sonny as he emerged through the fake fireplace.

They retired to Henri's makeshift office cordoned off by a red silk drape, separating it from the main library and intended for private meetings to plan attacks against the hated enemy.

"All of us want revenge for the brutal torture the SS and Gestapo committed on our people to reveal our identities, and for what they did to the little girl Charlène," Henri said.

"What shall we do?" Sonny asked.

"We have designed a plan to capture the bloody butcher himself, the Sturmbannführer!" Henri declared.

"How?" Marie asked.

"Sturmbannführer Gustav visits the tavern at 7 p.m. for dinner every Tuesday like clockwork. The Allied bombing raid will take place at 11 p.m. My plan is to tie him to a tree and make him watch as the Polish bombers burn the Nazi garrison to ashes before he dies a very unpleasant death," Henri said.

The night of Tuesday, May 23rd, 1944 was humid. The moon was at its lowest, a blessing to the partisan group.

Sturmbannführer Gustav entered the inn at his usual time, 7 p.m., with an arrogant swagger, announcing his arrival and demanding his nourishment from the innkeepers, Françoise and his wife Imogene, who by this time were quick to expect the Nazi's needs.

Outside, the Sturmbannführer's driver and bodyguard leaned against the Nazi staff car, MP 40s slung across their backs, smoking and joking, unaware of several men crouched in the shadows, knives drawn.

Henri waited with Sergio and the stable boy upstairs in an unlit corner of the hallway leading to guest bedrooms of the inn and tavern, fingering the clubs they carried.

Downstairs in the main dining room, the Sturmbannführer had an unexpected but pleasant surprise: a beautiful French girl was staying at the inn and was eating her supper at a nearby table. Her raiment was that of the poor, but she was beautiful, with bright blue eyes and translucent skin framed by a blue-black bob tucked into a chic felt hat.

The lovely French woman's shapely figure also caught Gustav's attention. He toasted her with his glass of wine, and she smiled, acknowledging his compliment. The Sturmbannführer invited her to join his table, provoking disgusted looks from other patrons in the inn.

"They are envious that I have your company, *oui?*" he asked.

"Perhaps," the young woman replied.

Over the next few hours, their conversation drifted from prewar outings in the country, to the beauty of Paris in the springtime, and the progress made by the German people in arts and science.

This evening is going well, the Sturmbannführer thought. *Who knows, maybe I will bed this lovely lady tonight!*

After several rounds of drinks, the French woman excused herself, "I must retire. I travel to Paris tomorrow to visit my aunt. Good night, Herr Gustav!"

He stood up, saying, "Have I done wrong, Mademoiselle? I was very much enjoying your company. Why must you leave so soon?"

"*Oui*, it was a most pleasant evening, Herr Sturmbannführer, but I have had too much to drink. Perhaps you could walk me to my room," the young woman said as she stood up, stumbling into his arms. The Sturmbannführer was lightheaded himself but had been careful not to drink too much, for what might follow a romantic dinner with the beautiful French woman.

Helping his dinner companion up the staircase, his arm wrapped around her waist, the lewd smirk on his face did not go unnoticed by Françoise, who whispered to Imogene, "That smirk won't be on his face for much longer," pinching her on the derriere as he passed by her to collect the dirty plates at the table the Nazi and French woman had vacated.

Outside, two SS soldiers lay in a pool of their own blood, as one partisan picked up a cigarette, taking a long drag. "You should try one, they are from Paris, *très bon*," as he kicked the body of the nearest Nazi.

The Sturmbannführer awoke to the salty taste of warm blood on his lips, a taste ingrained in his memory from his boxing days. His vision was blurred, and his head hurt. He could not move his arms and legs and he shook his head, attempting to clear his vision.

As he gained consciousness, he realized he was no longer at the inn and tavern, but somewhere in a wooded area, tied to a tree. Four men stood in front of him. He recognized them. There was that boy, Sonny, and his father, Henri.

The Sturmbannführer's eyes opened wide when he realized that the fourth person standing in front of him was not a man but the beautiful French woman he had walked back to her room at the inn. She was dressed in black trousers and a gray tunic, her hair tucked into a black beret.

"What is this? Release me now, or I will reduce your village to rubble! How dare you treat an officer of the Schutzstaffel this way?"

Henri responded with a wicked slap across the face. "Shut your mouth *vous cochon* and watch as we burn your precious garrison to the ground," Henri said.

"What are you talking about, Frenchman? By whom? Your humble Army?" the Sturmbannführer asked. Henri slapped him again.

Just then they made out the inimitable drone of aircraft engines approaching from across the ocean. The group watched as the de Havilland DH.98 Mosquito bomber group approached, searchlights illuminating the sky. The harsh sounds of Ack-Ack guns filled the air with their steady staccato of hot lead.

"Sturmbannführer, the Polish pilots volunteered for this mission to give *vous cochon* a taste of your own poison," Henri said, sounding almost mad with delirium.

The Sturmbannführer stood pinned against the tree, stunned by what he was seeing. In a panic, he began yelling for help. Henri was quick to silence him, stuffing a handkerchief in his mouth. He then tied a small rope with a knot, placed it in the Sturmbannführer's mouth, and tied the ends against the back of the Nazi's head. "That should keep him quiet," Henri said.

They now turned all eyes to the northwest as Mosquitos from the Polish 307th squadron passed overhead; Sonny felt as he could almost touch them; they seemed to graze the treetops. They were strategic night fighters developed for the RAF and used in such critical missions as pinpoint attacks on prisoner-of-war camps, Gestapo or German intelligence, and security force bases. This time, it was the Führer Adolf Hitler's divisional barracks they were bombing.

The Polish bomber group was still a few minutes away when colored marker flares appeared in the night sky. The partisans had marked the target. Intense flak broke out in the distance as the bombers approached the barracks and neighboring marshaling yards. Amidst the flares and the flashing explosions of bombs dropped by the DH.98 Mosquitos, Sonny and Henri felt the earth rumble underneath, even though they were far removed from the target.

The bombers descended to less than 500 feet, as the flak became thicker, and the shells burst all around the Mosquitos. The bombardier got busy.

Bombs away! Flak burst all around the incoming aircraft. The Mosquito's dropped incendiary and standard explosive five-hundred-pound bombs. Massive explosions followed by brightly burning flames.

Even from this distance, Sonny could see that bombs were still being showered down on the target. One bomber did a great service to the others by dropping his bomb load on a flak position, silencing the anti-aircraft gun. A starboard engine of one DH.98 Mosquito began to smoke and then flames appeared on the #1 engine. As the engine sputtered, the crew cut off the gasoline supply and feathered the engine, flying away on the plane's remaining engine.

The bomber crash-landed in a pea field; a Maquis partisan group rescued the crew, and eventually they were to return to England.

As the attack continued, Henri returned to the SS Sturmbannführer, still tied to a tree. He motioned for Marie, Sergio, and Sonny to join him. Sonny and Marie each held a hand grenade. Sonny and Henri pulled the pins; Marie took her grenade and placed it in the Sturmbannführer's tunic. She then grabbed the grenade from Sonny's hand and dropped it in the Sturmbannführer's trousers.

The team backed away, hearing the Sturmbannführer screaming through his garrote. The air vibrated as the grenades exploded into the night, blinding them. They heard strange thudding noises as body parts of the SS Sturmbannführer landed around them.

In the distance, smoke and flames from the demolished SS barracks lit up the night. Not a single German escaped.

Revenge was complete.

"Charlène, your torturer is dead. He can never hurt you again, little one," Sonny said, speaking to the universe.

Homeward

Sonny's brain was spinning faster than a turbine engine. He had seen more death and destruction in the past few weeks than he had ever seen in the movies. The SS and Gestapo brutalized a little girl. He killed two SS soldiers and took part in executing the Sturmbannführer.

Sonny knew in his heart that *this* was war. He had already learned there are no real victories in war. When one side wins, the other side mourns their lost loved ones, and vice versa. All the bloodshed Sonny witnessed made him sick to his stomach.

He had come to France a young teenager eager for war. He had arrived with the voracious appetite for a good home cooking. Just weeks later, Sonny was a sad, pensive young man who didn't touch his food, too morose to eat.

As Sonny was picking at his breakfast the next morning at the farmhouse, Henri approached him with an urgent look on his face.

"Sonny, I have received word from Major Smythe that a double agent has compromised your identity, Henri said. "I have arranged for transportation for you to leave tonight."

"Why must I leave so soon? I still have so much to do here before the invasion," Sonny protested.

"*Mon ami*, you *must* leave. The Nazis know your identity and are hunting you down. You are not safe here and you are no good to anybody dead. You have done the work you came to do—you assembled and delivered your radios. Pack your things; you leave tonight."

Sonny knew better than to argue. He had learned that Henri's word was final. Henri had been a sergeant in the French Army and had never accepted the surrender of his beloved France. He was an idealized local hero akin to Robin Hood or Rob Roy; the stuff of legends.

As he packed, Sonny felt an urgency to see home again, to sleep in his own bed instead of a cot in the farmhouse basement. For a moment he was hungry again as he thought about his mom's bacon, eggs and toast.

Sonny spent the day saying goodbye to the partisans, who slapped his back, urging him to return when the war was over. He gave detailed instructions to anyone who would listen about how to deal with radio problems. They had all heard Sonny's repair speech countless times, but they listened again, smiling. The emotion in the farmhouse was unanimous: *we will miss this fine young man.*

Marie and Sergio had left early that morning to gather intelligence on the V-2 rocket site near Watten. Sonny wondered if he would be able to say goodbye to them before he left.

Just after 6 p.m., as Sonny sat at the inn, pushing his dinner around on the plate, a wounded partisan burst into the tavern, asking for Henri. Françoise, the innkeeper, ushered the man into the kitchen, motioning for Henri to follow. Sonny left his table and peeked inside the kitchen. He could hear the men whispering. Henri's head dropped; he grasped the shoulder of the innkeeper as if he would fall to the ground without support.

Henri instructed the partisan to have a seat on the bench in the kitchen while he went to the cellar to get supplies to clean and dress the man's wounds. The partisan looked up and gave Sonny a sorrowful glance before looking away.

Sonny sat in silence for more than an hour while Henri tended to the partisan's wounds. Françoise and Imogene came to his table to encourage Sonny to eat, to no avail.

"Sonny, please come here," Henri said. "I have horrible news for you, *mon ami.*"

Sonny's stomach heaved.

It must be Marie or Sergio or both, he thought.

"*The Bosch* ambushed Marie today near the village of Watten. She died, but not before she took out many of our enemies. I'm so sorry, son. I know how fond you were of Marie," Henri said.

"How did this happen?" Sonny asked.

"By the time Major Smythe informed me of the double agent, she was already on her mission. I could do nothing to save her."

Sonny could not hold back the sobs as Henri grasped him in a bear hug, holding him as Sonny went limp in his arms. Those watching would have seen tears fall from Henri's eyes.

"What about Sergio?" Sonny asked through his tears.

"The partisan who came here tonight says he saw Sergio being hoisted onto a German truck. That's all we know at the moment," Henri said.

At about 10 p.m., Sonny and Henri returned to the farmhouse. Henri instructed Sonny to pack while he checked on the farm animals. That evening Sonny tried to concentrate on the good things in his life; his mother, brothers and sister and friends, but his memories of Marie, Henri, and Antoinette, whom he thought of as an extended family, always came to the forefront. He found it hard to push back the tears.

As he sat on his cot, packed gear at his feet, Henri appeared in the cellar doorway. "Time to go, Sonny. The courier plane coming in from England will be at the rendezvous point within an hour and you must board. It will drop off supplies after landing and takeoff afterwards, with or without you. We must leave now; we are out of time."

"*Oui*," was the only response Sonny could muster. He rose from the cot and grabbed his gear. With a final glance around his basement "bedroom," he walked up the stairs.

As Sonny entered the farmhouse kitchen, Antoinette was waiting for him, tears streaming down her face. She handed

Sonny a small parcel of food for his trip, wrapped as usual in a large cloth napkin. She hugged him, kissed both cheeks, and wished him, "*Au revoir*, and Godspeed, *mon infant.*"

Sonny thanked Antoinette and promised he would return soon after the war ended, because he couldn't live without her company and her cooking.

Outside, Henri waited with a pair of horses. Henri smiled as he noted, "This is the best transport we can get in these times."

"Finest in France, *Papa*," Sonny said.

They both mounted and rode off on the familiar path they had traveled many times before. Within minutes, two Communist Maquis partisans flagged them down.

"You cannot travel on this path. The Nazis have patrols along this route."

"How many?" Henri inquired.

"They have an entire company out there, Henri," came the reply.

A third partisan approached the horses, brandishing a German Luger.

"Get off of your horses and lay flat on the ground or I will shoot him first," he said, pointing at Sonny. "Dead or alive, it doesn't matter, but you both are worth more alive to the Gestapo."

Sonny's blood boiled as he recognized the thick Spanish accent of the third man. It was Sergio! He was the double agent working for the Nazis.

That bastard led the SS to Charlène and our team, Sonny thought. *That's why Henri was so intent on getting me out of the area.*

Sonny's spurred his horse.

"Over my dead body will you get us, dead or alive, you bastard," he yelled at Sergio.

Sonny jerked the reins of his horse, causing the mare to buck up, legs kicking. The horse kicked a partisan in the head, killing him. Sergio fired a shot just as Henri's horse trampled him. The shot rang out into the still quiet night.

Sonny and Henri looked at each other in horror. The German patrols would investigate. Worse yet, one partisan was missing.

"Sonny, that was excellent. Thanks to your actions, we will live to fight one more day," Henri said.

"I just reacted," Sonny said.

"We have to move now, *mon ami*; they will be on us at any moment," Henri said, urging his horse forward.

"What do you suggest? Is there another path we can take?" Sonny asked.

"*Oui*, follow me," Henri said.

They moved back along the dirt trail towards the main road that led in and out of town on an east-west axis. The trail they were on ran north-south and the field in which the plane would land was in the southeast.

Henri turned his horse to the right and headed down the main road heading east. Sonny followed in hot pursuit. As they put some distance from the trail, Sonny began to feel more comfortable. It was common knowledge that the Germans patrolled the main road day and night but stayed off the trails to avoid encounters with the partisan groups in the area. This was a necessity since they watched the trail. It was a necessary but dangerous detour.

Sonny's sadness over Marie had boiled over in a rage when his horse kicked Sergio. His mind now swirled with images of their time together and he suppressed feelings of betrayal.

No time for that now, he thought.

Henri slowed his horse to a stop and motioned to Sonny to move off into a wooded area, while putting his finger to his pursed lips. They dismounted and walked into the woods with their horses in tow as they heard the clacking noise of a tracked vehicle just ahead in the darkness.

The German 15th Army had been moving troops around at night in the Pas-de-Calais in the two preceding weeks to keep them from aerial reconnaissance. The heightened Nazi presence in the area made partisan operations very difficult. It was a double-edged sword, they wanted to fool the Nazis into occupying the area, away from Normandy, but it put them in German gun sights. During this period in the war, the partisans only gathered information about troop movements in the area. British intelligence advised partisan groups not to attack German troop movements, or destroy the German army's infrastructure, because of revenge tactics used by the SS units throughout France.

Sonny and Henri waited in the woods as German Panzers and halftracks clanged by. Their efforts to keep their horses quiet failed when Sonny's horse whinnied at the horrible sounds made by the halftrack. Both men stood frozen, relieved when none of the soldiers marching near the halftrack investigated the horse's sounds. Sonny mused that maybe the soldiers ignored animal sounds in the countryside.

Sonny and Henri held their breath as they watched a soldier walking through the woods towards them. The soldier relieved himself and looked back to see if they had noticed him leaving the column. It had been a long march and he couldn't wait any longer. But he didn't unzip his fly. The cold steel of Henri's knife sliced the soldier's neck moments later. The man fell to the ground, choking on his own blood.

Henri was back to Sonny in an instant, moving away from the body in the familiar woods.

"Back to the trail," he whispered as he grabbed his horse's reins from Sonny and led them deeper into the forest. After a few hundred yards they came across the trail they had left and proceeded southeast to their destination.

"We lost valuable time on our unfortunate detour," Henri commented. "The pilot won't wait long, but we can still make it in time."

"I can always stay, Henri", Sonny commented, reluctant to leave Henri in danger.

Sonny longed to go home. The events of the past few weeks had disturbed him.

How I hate this war, he thought. *I can't imagine how once all I wanted was to be a war hero, making up stories with Raymond on the rooftop of our duplex, and bragging about how we saved the day.*

Now Sonny vowed he would never tell another war story as long as he lived. Many veterans like Sonny made the same vow, unable to tell their families and friends what they endured.

The unmistakable sounds of shouts signaled that the Germans had discovered the body of the dead SS soldier.

"We have no more time for stealth, Sonny. Ride hard; the enemy is at our backs!" Henri shouted as he took off with a gallop.

A few minutes later, they entered a small clearing and noticed the dark silhouette of a small two-seater plane, its engine humming in readiness. Behind them, trucks, tanks, motorcycles, and shouting grew louder.

Henri knew that the *Boche* were quick and vengeful when partisans killed one of their own. *We only have a few precious moments before our enemy is upon us*, Henri thought.

As the horses approached the plane, two German soldiers appeared on motorcycles at the outskirts of the field and opened fire on Henri and Sonny.

Sonny felt a thump as his horse shuddered and fell to the ground, convulsing as it died from the bullet wounds. Trapped under his dying horse, Sonny tried to free himself, with no success. Meanwhile, Henri had dismounted, striking his horse on its rear to send it galloping away to safety.

Henri dropped to one knee. He took aim with his MAS Modèle 36 rifle, which he had used since he was a sergeant in the French Army and put a bullet into an approaching soldier's head. The other soldier dove for cover behind a fallen tree and sprayed the area with his MP 40 submachine gun.

Henri pulled Sonny out from under his dead horse at the same time the pilot threw open the passenger door of the plane, screaming "Get in now!" above the noise of the engine.

"Henri, come with us, you'll die if you stay here," Sonny said.

"No, *mon ami*, my place is here, alive or dead. As long as I breathe, I have to fight for the freedom of my beloved France. Now get on that plane! *Viva La Resistance*, Sonny!" he shouted.

"I'll be back Henri, I promise!" Sonny shouted back.

Just then, another group of soldiers appeared at the wood line, firing at the courier plane. Bullets streaked by, one exploding in Henri's leg, just as Sonny closed the plane's passenger door. He tried reopening the door, but the pilot grabbed his hand away from the latch while shoving the throttle forward as the plane rocked on the rough ground.

Henri dropped to one knee, the pain coursing through his leg. *So, is this the way I will go?* he wondered.

He glanced at the plane and saw Sonny screaming his name and yelling, "Get out of there!"

Turning to the pilot Sonny pleaded, "Turn around! Henri needs our help!"

"No, Sonny," the British pilot remarked, "I have explicit directions from Major Smythe and Henri to get you out of here, no matter what. With luck and God's blessing, Henri will live to tell you a jolly good tale. That chap has nine lives. He'll be alive for another rendezvous with Jerry."

The plane lurched upward into the pitch-black sky as bullets made a tapping noise on its tail rudder.

On the ground, Henri saw the enemy approach. He took two hand grenades from his ammo belt and pulled the pins.

"I see Der Führer has sent his finest to me," he shouted in German as they came closer.

"Come and get me, *vous cochons!*" he yelled, as two hand grenades flew from his hands.

Sonny sat in silence on the uneventful flight to England. In just a month, he had gone from a spirited apprentice to a hardened veteran.

At first, he despised the pilot for leaving Henri, but realized that going back would have been futile. Besides, Henri would not have wanted Sonny captured or killed. Henri had been like a father to Sonny.

"I will live my life making you and Charlène proud," Sonny said. "I'll always take care of people and children in need."

Hours later the plane made an almost perfect landing on the airfield in Bungay, England.

Weeks later on a sunny Saturday morning, Joe walked through the front door of his New Hampshire home. He was in his State Guard uniform, ditty bag thrown over his shoulder. His sister Louise was the first to greet him.

"Did you catch any Japs in the cornfields, Joe?" she asked.

"Don't be silly," Joe said.

"Well, if you didn't, it looks like you will get the chance," Louise said. "There's an official-looking telegram with your name on it. I had to sign for it."

"You're kidding, right?" he asked.

"Nope," she said as she waltzed into the kitchen to get some coffee. "Want a cup?" she asked popping her head around the kitchen door.

"Sure," Joe said as he tossed his bag over his shoulder and onto the floor.

Joe's mother rushed down the stairs. Before she walked down the hallway towards him, she rubbed her hands on her apron and checked her hair in the mirror, straightening her dress as she always did. She gave Joe a big hug and kisses, which had always embarrassed him in the past, but this time he responded in kind, holding his mother close for a long time.

After the events of the past few weeks, Joe realized how much he had missed his family.

"Nice to be home, Mom!" He said.

"Glad to have you home, Sonny," she replied.

"What's cookin'?" he asked, smelling the bacon on the stove.

The front door burst open and Raymond hugged Joe.

"So glad we are both home," he said.

Nosy neighbors walking by Joe's house that morning would have witnessed a familiar scene: the family sitting down to bacon and eggs, passing food to each other, laughing and teasing. Joe's mom looked at her youngest.

My Sonny-boy has become a man, she thought.

Raymond stared at Joe, too. *He looks like he aged 15 years in the past few months. I wonder if he's ill.*

Later that day Joe relaxed on the back-porch swing. He smiled as he watched the neighborhood children race to the tracks to watch and wave as the three o'clock freight train passed by.

Not so long ago, I did that, he thought. *Guess I should read the telegram.*

Joe opened his telegram from the government.

Greetings from the President of the United States, you are hereby ordered to report for your pre-induction physical..."

Let's Finish This

Joe arrived at the address given to him by Gisele. He knew this area of town but hadn't been this way in a long time. It had become run down; one of the least desirable areas to live. *Makes sense, people will leave you alone here and mind their own business*, Joe thought.

He parked his car a block away and started to walk towards the house. On the way, he passed some young punks who hopped off their porch and walked alongside him, asking if he had any money.

"Get lost," Joe growled.

One teen pulled out a knife and put it to Joe's ear. "Seems like you're the one who's lost, old man."

"You kids these days," Joe complained as he flashed his pistol and knocked off the teen's hat. "I said get lost."

"We don't want any trouble, mister," the teen said. The group backed away to their porch.

Joe pushed his pistol back into his shoulder holster under his coat and continued to walk towards the house. As he walked up the pathway, the front door creaked open.

How melodramatic, Joe thought as he pushed the door open a little wider. As he entered, he felt a pistol barrel against the back of his head and stiffened, waiting for the shot to come.

"Not yet, Sonny. Drop your pistol on the floor," Gisele ordered as she closed the front door and motioned with her gun for Joe to get into the middle of the room. Joe started to remove his pistol from his left shoulder with his right hand, hoping to get a shot off.

"No, use your other hand," Gisele barked. Joe removed the pistol with his left hand. *No chance for that shot now*, he grimaced in disgust.

"Hands behind you, Sonny. Try nothing, or your daughter-in-law is dead," Gisele warned.

"Are you letting Emily go, trading my life for hers as we agreed?" Joe asked Gisele as she cuffed his hands behind his back.

"I will keep my bargain; even though killing her first in front of you would be awful, wouldn't it?" Gisele said, laughing.

"Keep your bargain. I have kept mine," Joe said.

"Tell me, just *who* are you, Gisele?" Joe asked.

"As if you don't know! *You* murdered my grandfather in 1944," Gisele replied.

"I have killed no one, Gisele. You must mistake me for someone else," Joe challenged.

"Don't lie to me," Gisele spat out, hitting Joe across the back of his head with the pistol butt. He fell to his knees.

"The Sturmbannführer you blew up in France…Remember now, Sonny?"

Joe forced himself to stay conscious; it took all he had to ask her how she had learned his identity.

"Torture works wonders! Former Gestapo agents taught me well when they found out I wanted to avenge my grandfather's murder. I researched the names of Allied veterans and worked my way across the country, identifying and ending them."

"You're doing all the talking, Gisele, or better yet—may I address you as *vous cochon?*"

"Enough!" Gisele shouted as she grabbed Joe by his jacket, pushing him forward towards the basement door. She kicked the door open, banging it against the cellar wall. She kicked Joe down the stairs. Halfway down, tumbling head over heels, Joe heard the crack of a bone and felt his right leg go numb. He landed with a thud at the base of the stairs.

Pain seared through his body and he struggled once again to remain conscious. *Whatever happens, stay awake and don't pass out*, Joe repeated to himself.

"Heinz, get the girl ready. I will get the car," Gisele announced. A short stocky German with dark hair threw Joe into the corner. Joe winced as the pain shot up his leg.

Heinz untied Emily from the chair and then retied her arms behind her and pushed her into a corner of the room next to her father-in-law.

Joe asked, "You okay?" *A ludicrous question given the circumstance,* he thought.

Emily nodded.

"We still have a chance, but you need to follow my lead, Emily," Joe whispered.

Heinz turned towards Joe.

"Be quiet old man, or I will make your death much more painful," Heinz warned.

He put pressure on Joe's broken leg with his heavy black military boot. Joe ground his teeth to bite back the pain shooting through his body.

Just at that moment, there was a knock at the cellar door at the other end of the basement. Heinz turned away from Joe and walked towards the door, just as a second, louder knock came from behind the door.

"I am coming, Gisele," he spoke in German, "*Bitte*."

Reaching for the doorknob, he pulled at it before he realized he had also bolted the door. Chuckling, he reached up to unlatch the bolt.

About ten minutes after midnight, Jack and his mother drove off in his Durango. Claire and Sonny had changed into jeans, black t-shirts, and sneakers. They drove for about thirty minutes before they came to the address in Newark and saw Joe's parked car.

As they got out, Claire tucked her pistol in a shoulder holster, not bothering to conceal it as Joe had done with his. Jack pulled out the shotgun from the back seat. The teenagers who had returned to their porch after Joe went into Gisele's house crept back into their house, catching Jack's attention.

"What's up with them?" he asked his mother.

"Oh, I don't know, maybe a pistol in my hand and that shotgun you're carrying might have something to do with it?"

"Oh yeah," he muttered.

As they approached the house Claire took Jack by the arm and held him back.

"Jack, I don't know what will happen in there, but I need to tell you this before we go inside. Many years ago, after the war, the Russian government sent me to spy on your father. But things worked out, because we fell in love with each other. I denounced the country of my birth and took asylum in the United States. Soon after that, we married. Your father knows none of this and if he is still alive, I want to be the one to tell him, is that clear?"

"Sure, Mom, but I have to tell you, it's been one hell of a year for family secrets coming out of the closet."

"Let's get going; your father needs our help," Claire said. "You stay out of sight in the front yard, don't let anyone leave this house," she ordered.

"Sure thing," Jack answered.

Jack hid behind a large bush near the front door, the shotgun tucked under his left arm. Claire ducked down below the window on the main floor to avoid being seen by anyone who might be in the house. At the rear of the house, Claire found exterior bulkhead doors made of old, peeling wood. She opened the right side to reveal a steel door at the bottom of the steps.

Claire crept down the steps closing the bulkhead door over her head. Once she was all the way inside, she listened for any sounds coming from the basement.

She heard the unmistakable voice of her husband, in pain, and gritted her teeth in anger. She heard a man say in a German accent: "Be quiet old man, or your death will be much more painful."

Claire had to act; time was running out. On impulse she knocked on the door.

Heinz opened the door to see a pistol pointed at his face. Claire pulled the trigger, but Heinz was quick. He grabbed her arm and her shot ricochet around the room, causing a deafening noise. Joe bent over Emily to protect her. The shot lodged into the side of an old desk in the room.

Claire struggled with the massive German who dwarfed her, and her pistol skittered across the room about halfway between Joe and her. Heinz tossed Claire away from him, moving towards the gun, but Claire pounced on him, biting a finger off of his hand as he reached for it. He screamed in pain as he punched Claire, knocking her unconscious.

Heinz picked up the 9 mm pistol and turned to face Joe, only to realize that Joe was behind him, swinging a steel pipe at his head. He got a round off, hitting Joe in the chest, seconds before the fatal blow from the rubber tube broke Heinz neck.

Joe crumpled to the ground, crawling over to Claire with what little strength he had left. The wound was fatal. Behind him Emily whimpered. Joe propped himself up against a wall. He cradled Claire's head in his arms. As he placed her head in his lap, she awoke, looking up at him. She tore open his shirt when she saw the blood oozing from his chest. As she started to put pressure on his wound with the wadded remnants of his shirt, he pushed her arm away. Claire dropped her head, and sobbing, lay cradled in his arms.

Jack was just settling into position behind the bushes when the front door opened and Gisele walked onto the porch. As she walked past, Jack said the first words that popped out of his mouth: "Hey Gisele, how's my wife?"

Gisele turned towards him and started to raise her pistol, but Jack was quicker and hit her square in the face with the butt of the shotgun, knocking Gisele out cold.

"Where's Gisele?" Joe asked Claire.

Footsteps echoed down into the basement. It was Jack.

"Tied up in the hallway closet," Jack rushing into the basement.

Emily lay in the corner. Jack ran over and removed the duct tape from her face and the rope tying her hands together. After they embraced and kissed, Jack started to help her up. But Emily shook her head and pointed to Joe.

"Jack…your father" was all Emily could say with a sob before Jack saw Joe's wound.

"Dad, come on, we've got to get you to the hospital," Jack said, moving towards his dad. But Joe held up his free arm. "No, this is all she wrote, son. I'm a goner."

Jack dropped to his knees beside his parents and Emily joined him.

"Nice job, Queenie," Joe complimented Claire. "You saved the kids," He coughed up blood.

"Joe be still," Claire said. "We need to get you to the hospital."

"It's too late," Joe said, touching her face.

"Please hold on Joe," Claire pleaded.

"Ever since our time in London, I have never regretted you in my life."

"From that moment on, I turned my back on the Russians and asked for asylum in America," Claire said. "I will always love you."

Joe turned to Jack. "Take care of your mother."

Joe's breath became shallow and slowed as he died with his blue eyes looking into Claire's tear-filled eyes.

Claire let out a howl like a wild animal in pain. Jack and Emily sat, stroking her hair.

After a few minutes, Claire closed Joe's eyes, kissed his forehead and laid a blanket over his body, whispering, "Good night my love."

The sun was rising on the horizon when Gisele awoke in the passenger seat of Jack's Durango. She tested the ropes constraining her, but they did not budge.

"Jack, what do you plan to do with me?" Gisele asked.

Not taking his eyes off the road ahead, Jack replied, "The same thing you did to all those American veterans."

"Let me go, Jack," Gisele pleaded in a childlike voice. "You can take me to the FBI, and I will turn myself in."

They were driving down a winding dirt road, but Gisele had no clue where they were. The dust creeping through the broken passenger door was choking Gisele, but all her pleading met with silence from Jack.

"Jack, where are you taking me?" Gisele asked.

"You'll see where we are going soon. Some call this road the Lover's Leap, because a few lovers have not paid attention to its winding curves and have driven off the cliffs to their deaths. Some locals claim that spirits of deceased lovers haunt these canyons, because they see lights flashing in the night," Jack said.

The Durango skidded to a stop, causing gravel and dirt to fly everywhere.

"We're here," Jack announced.

Joe untied the rope holding the door shut. He unbuckled Gisele's seat belt.

"What's *here*?" Gisele asked. "Just turn me in Jack, I can provide valuable information to your government."

"I cannot allow that," Jack said looking beyond her to the 400-foot deep chasm below. "Goodbye, *vous cochon*."

Jack gunned the Durango and propelled it into a sharp U-turn. The truck catapulted Gisele from her seat and she rolled into the chasm. Her screams lasted for a few moments. A loud thud interrupted the silence at the bottom of the canyon.

"I've gotta get that door fixed," Jack said. "Someone could get hurt."

A Cold Morning

The snows fell on a cold January morning.

Jack parked the car on the far end of the cemetery parking lot. He walked along the path towards Sonny's grave. He enjoyed the walk, always feeling comforted by the sound of running water and the angels, stallions, and cherubs that circled the old fountain.

Jack trudged to his Dodge Durango, deep in thought, oblivious to the man dressed in black standing behind two maple trees or the shiny black limousine that circled the cemetery's perimeter road and stopped at the ice-encrusted pathway leading to Sonny's headstone.

The limousine driver opened the passenger door.

A woman, in her seventies, wearing a black suit, white three-quarter gloves, and silver beret covering salt and pepper curls, emerged from the limousine, dropping smart black leather boots to the pavement. She declined the driver's help, leaning on a cane in her left hand. She reached into the limousine seat; and retrieved a cashmere gray coat.

She stood there for several moments, touching the patch over her left eye with a white-gloved hand, as if wiping away hidden tears. Looking down at the icy pathway leading to Sonny's grave, she stiffened, noticing fresh boot marks.

Why must I always be in danger, even when I'm paying my respects to the dead? she thought.

The woman surveyed the cemetery grounds. She whispered to the driver, and he, too, looked around the cemetery grounds. He implored her to return to the limousine.

After a few moments, she stepped forward toward Sonny's headstone.

The limousine driver stepped to the side as she moved forward, eager to lend a hand in the slippery conditions. The woman waved him away with an annoyed glance. He returned to stand at attention at the limousine's rear passenger door, awaiting her return.

The woman limped on the snow-covered cobblestone pathway to Sonny's headstone, her right arm dangling from the weight of her coat. Stopping in front of Sonny's grave, she removed the white leather glove from her left hand with her teeth; placing her hand on the headstone and bowed in prayer.

A few minutes passed before the woman bent down on her left knee, holding the headstone. She kissed the headstone, a single tear dropping to the ground.

"Sonny, oh Sonny, who will take care of me now? Now that you're gone, will they kill me too?" she asked.

She looked back and motioned to the driver. He reached into the front passenger floor of the limousine and pulled out a florist box that held a beautiful crystal vase with forty-four red roses, and a handwritten card tucked amid the thorns. The driver placed the vase at the foot of the headstone and went back to the limousine with the florist's box in his hand.

The women then leaned down to scrape and mound the snow around the flower vase to keep it from falling in the wind. She rearranged the roses and reattached the gift card to the plastic pick.

Jack surveyed the scene in silence as he stood beside his Durango in the cemetery parking lot. He had been the only visitor parked in the lot and was about to open his car with his key fob when he saw a limousine pull up to his father's grave.

He saw an old woman with a cane, with an obvious limp in her right leg and a patch over her left eye, kneel at his dad's grave.

What the hell? Jack thought. *Just who is this woman? She wasn't at Dad's funeral.*

The woman cried at his father's headstone. *My dad must have meant a lot to her,* Jack thought. *But I've never met her. The woman looks like she'd be about 10 years younger than dad. She looks chic, French, like a petite Jacqueline Kennedy. French!*

Jack raced through the parking lot to his father's grave just as the limousine was pulling away. Several rose petals floated onto the pathway. The gift card was lying in front of the vase. Jack picked up the red petals and rubbed them between his fingertips. He read at the card.

Thank you for keeping your promise to take care of me, Sonny.

My love always, Charlène.

Acknowledgments

To my wife Kim, for patiently listening.

Thank you, Gary Deslauriers, for the beautiful cover art.

About the Author

Ken graduated from Norwich University in Vermont in 1980 and spent 13 years in military service in the Army, leaving at the rank of Major. During this time, he served as a company commander during Desert Shield and Desert Storm, earning the Bronze Star, Kuwait Liberation Medal and Combat Air Medal.